Richard Gordon was born in 1921. He qua... on to work as an anaesthetist at St Bartholomew's Hospital, and then as a ship's surgeon. As obituary-writer for the *British Medical Journal*, he was inspired to take up writing full-time and he left medical practice in 1952 to embark on his 'Doctor' series. This proved incredibly successful and was subsequently adapted into a long-running television series.

Richard Gordon has produced numerous novels and writings, all characterised by his comic tone and remarkable powers of observation. His *Great Medical Mysteries* and *Great Medical Discoveries* concern the stranger aspects of the medical profession whilst his *The Private Life of…*series takes a deeper look at individual figures within their specific medical and historical setting. Although an incredibly versatile writer, he will, however, probably always be best-known for his creation of the hilarious 'Doctor' series.

The Captain's Table

Richard Gordon

This edition published in 2001 by House of Stratus, an imprint of Stratus Books Ltd., 21 Beeching Park, Kelly Bray, Cornwall, PL17 8QS, UK.

www.houseofstratus.com

Typeset, printed and bound by House of Stratus.

A catalogue record for this book is available from the British Library and the Library of Congress.

ISBN 1-84232-494-2

1

Captain William Ebbs, MBE, Master of the Pole Star Line freighter *Martin Luther*, looked gloomily through the rain into the lower windows of his Company's office in Leadenhall Street. They were bright with shiny models of liners, sliced miniature cabins, coloured photographs of bronzing girls leaping for deck quoits, and sunny posters beckoning bronchitic Englishmen *Come to Australia!* – a cheerful picture of ship-board life which always upset him. So did the office itself, where every Captain was summoned in the fresh insignificance of his shore-going clothes, to be bullied by pale clerks or girlish secretaries and asked fogging questions about storm damage, sick seamen, and condemned stores reported and forgotten long ago in the voyage. These official visits had for many years seemed to Ebbs the severest penalties of command; but his present arrival was more heavily overshadowed by the certainty that he had come ashore to be sacked.

Ebbs was a tall, bony, mild-eyed man with fussy hands and awkward feet, a distortion of the conventional image of a ship's Captain, who now bore his authority with the weary air of an underpaid schoolmaster on the last day of term. As he entered the building he respectfully removed his weeping trilby, misshapen through long stowage in sea air and nibbled by a hundred insects unknown in English wardrobes, and revealed under his mackintosh a brown tweed suit that had apparently been used for storing potatoes.

'But Sir Angus was expecting you all the afternoon, Captain!' said the girl inside, as he announced himself.

'I'm afraid I was delayed at the dock. How is he?' he added as though asking if the blade were sharp.

1

'He seems rather out of sorts today, sir.'

Speculating briskly on the possibilities of shore employment, Ebbs followed her to the room where the Chairman of the Line sat among the teak and traditions of his former ships.

The Pole Star Company was founded in the 1850s by a red-bearded Orkney sea-captain called Andrew McWhirrey, who had roared his way around the China coast for forty years and by not troubling overmuch about working men and ships to death sailed into a fortune. He was a pious sailor, who screwed his personal indulgence down to a pipeful of tobacco at sunset and carried a Bible under his arm like a telescope. 'The harvest truly is plenteous, but the labourers are few!' he would shout at an idle deckhand, kicking him headlong into the scuppers; 'Abstain from fleshly lusts, which war against the soul!' he could roar at a drunken bos'n, knocking him over the poop rail. Drinking and gambling were forbidden in his ship, and every Sunday all hands were ordered aft for Church; he had a fine voice for reading prayers, and it was said that no one could take a better burial at sea.

The present head of the Line was an attenuated form of old Andrew, whose portrait stared down with a salty eye from the wall. The fiery hair was reduced to a pair of fuzzy hedges on a pink scalp, the eyes that once split horizons were diluted with spectacles, and the voice that roared bloody threats into the fo'c'sle modulated politely for the telephone. But Angus McWhirrey was as tough a shipowner as his great-grandfather. As he could no longer use a belaying-pin or his boots he subjected his subordinates with daily lashes of confidential memoranda, which vetoed promotion and kept men he disliked in the Company's outdated tramps until they were overtaken by retirement or heat-stroke.

For some seconds McWhirrey looked at Ebbs in the way his ancestor used to inspect errant members of the crew while deciding whether to flog them at the main-mast or blacken their faces with boiling pitch.

'Sit down, Captain,' he said quietly.

Ebbs obediently took the edge of a chair.

'Your report from Aden,' McWhirrey went on, 'contains many interesting passages. I am particularly struck by your remark...' He found his place on the flimsy. '"The *Martin Luther* is no longer fit for the conveyance of freight, animals, or sailors, and I recommend that she be scrapped, scuttled, or when next in Australia presented to the Government for the detonation of atomic bombs."' He looked up. 'Would you care to expand that, Captain? Just take your time. I have the whole afternoon to listen to anyone who knows more about the shipping business than myself.'

Ebbs felt the rain on his collar begin to soak down his neck, and said nothing.

For five years he had held impatient command of the *Martin Luther*, a long, low, hag of a ship creaking herself to a standstill across the oceans of the world. He had dutifully suffered her uncertain refrigeration that left the food suddenly rotten and rancid a week out of port; the electric light that dimmed and faltered nightly; the condensation that streamed down the cabin bulkheads and the cockroaches which paraded up them; the bewildering steering engine that set the ship cutting perilous circles in Sydney harbour; and the crew of malcontents, refused by a dozen masters of better vessels, who came every morning truculently to the bridge and generally ended their shore-leave in handcuffs. But the complaints that came hotly from his pen, kennelled in his cabin in the detachment of another hemisphere, froze and perished in the London air: he knew that the Pole Star Line expected its captains to fret in honourable silence.

'I was perhaps a little overwrought,' he murmured hopefully. 'The heat, Sir Angus...'

'We do not expect our masters, who are in charge of lives and ships in tropical waters, to be affected by the heat like girl guides on a picnic.'

Ebbs rose. He could at least take his dismissal like a master mariner of the British Merchant Marine.

'Sir Angus,' he said with dignity. 'I have given twenty-five years of my life to this Company – since I was a cadet of sixteen, and in a far better ship than the *Martin Luther* I may say. I have always done my duty strictly in the Company's interests, as my father and my grandfather did before me. I had hoped that in time virtue would not have to be its own reward, but I see that I was mistaken. As you no longer require my services, I will say good day to you, sir.' He replaced his hat with modest defiance. 'I am now going out to find myself a job. What or where, I have not the slightest idea, but at least it will be a change from the Pole Star Company. Who, I might tell

3

you, Sir Angus,' he continued, feeling a little alarmed at himself, 'are the biggest bunch of robbers afloat since Captain Kidd. Good afternoon!'

'Captain Ebbs,' McWhirrey said patiently. 'You sometimes appear to be a bloody fool.'

Ebbs paused.

'It's not a question of dismissing you. I asked you here to promote you.' He pointed with his pencil to a rack on the wall like a train indicator, which reproduced the daily position of the Pole Star fleet. In one column were the fast white liners, which inherited their titles like aristocrats, enjoyed launchings like fashionable weddings, and had their movements recorded below the stock market in *The Times*; in the other, the fifty hard-worked unknown cargo boats, that crept from British ports with ensigns humbled to their big sisters to lose themselves for months at a time among the sweaty harbours of the Java Sea, the Persian Gulf, or the Queensland coast. 'You knew Captain Buckle was taken ill?'

Ebbs stared at him.

'Collapsed on the bus yesterday. A great pity, of course. Nevertheless, his ship still has to sail for Sydney on Monday. And we haven't a relief. We are therefore appointing you to the *Charlemagne*, Captain.'

'But she's a passenger ship!'

'So I was aware when my wife launched her.'

Ebbs struggled for coherence, swallowed, and stopped. Instead he blew his nose. He often did so to make a point, seize time to think, or relieve emotion.

'When can you go aboard?' Sir Angus asked.

'Tonight – any time – this minute, if necessary.'

'Tomorrow morning will be soon enough.' McWhirrey got up and paced thoughtfully across floorboards once trodden by a generation of angry shipmasters. 'Captain Ebbs, what makes you think we people in the office know nothing at all that goes on at sea? Of course the *Luther's* a bad ship. That's precisely why we kept you there. I'm not in the habit of handing out bouquets, but you made a good job of her – in your own way. At least you kept the vessel going and the crew alive, which is something of an achievement in the *Luther*. You must have more confidence in yourself, man! You're not a fourth mate any more. And try not to be so infernally fussy. It'll only upset your new officers.'

'Fussy? Me fussy, sir?'

'I must make it quite clear that this new appointment is probationary. I gather Buckle's unlikely to return to sea. If you're a success we may therefore consider a permanency, despite your views on the company that pays you – '

'I meant it only…only as a joke.' Ebbs tried to smile.

'No doubt. Most amusing. With ordinary luck, and if you find your feet early enough, there's no reason why you shouldn't make a perfectly good Captain in the *Charlemagne*. But if you're not a success – back to the *Martin Luther*. You understand?'

Ebbs nodded.

'Very well. Then there seems nothing more for me to do except congratulate you on behalf of the directors. And of course wish you a most pleasant voyage.'

2

In the Royal Navy a new Captain enjoys a stimulating welcome to his ship in a ceremony shrill with bo's'n's pipes and aflutter with salutes; but in the Merchant Service – even in such a courtly section of it as the Pole Star Line – his arrival is as unexciting as the appearance of a new stationmaster.

Early the next morning Ebbs arrived at Tilbury and stood on the quay, anonymous in his mackintosh, looking at the chilly white sides of the *Charlemagne* with the excitement of a cadet spotting his first ship. It had been his ambition to command a passenger liner since he had curled in his hammock as an unpleasantly spotty adolescent in the training vessel *Worcester*. Even his first sickly voyage and his first seagoing Captain – a booming six-footer who made his crew feel that the arrival of the Day of Judgement would now be something of an anticlimax – had not quenched his confidence of ascending with maturity to the bridge of a mail steamer. At twenty he had excitedly found himself appointed Third Mate of a Pole Star Liner, and as he was a thoughtful young man who smuggled aboard books on training the mind instead of pornography he drew up a secret scheme to lead him to the comfort of a captain's cabin. He would do all the unsavoury tasks like checking the lifeboats and inspecting the bilge pumps, and report them to the Chief Officer as completed; he would ballast his slight sea-going experience with heavy reading from the *Manual of Seamanship*; and he would watch constantly for irregularities in the ship's structure and routine, informing the Captain while he took his daily walk alone before breakfast. This system led to Ebbs being thrown out of the ship at the end of the voyage, but discouragement settled on him only as he began to see the years repel his goal: from Third Mate in a ship carrying a dozen passengers he was promoted to Second Officer in another with only three, to Chief Officer in a meat ship with no passengers at all, and lastly to be Captain of the *Martin Luther*, where his ambitions rapidly withered in her hot hull to aspiring command of any vessel with predictable steering.

Ebbs rapidly climbed the long gangway to the *Charlemagne's* after-deck.

'Good morning,' he said to the fat Quartermaster at the top. 'I'm the Captain.'

'No you ain't,' he said guardedly. 'The Captain's sick.'

'The new Captain,' Ebbs explained.

The man awarded him a sluggish salute.

'Is the Chief Officer aboard?'

The Quartermaster screwed up his eyes. 'Chief Officer, sir? No, sir. Not on board, sir. On leave.'

'Well, how about the Second Officer?'

'Ah, I know where he is. Ashore at the dentist's. The Purser's with the Customs, the Chief Steward's down at the catering department, the Doctor don't generally show up till sailing day, and the Chief Engineer's turned in with a bad cold. Orders not to be disturbed, sir.'

'Who's keeping ship?' Ebbs said sharply.

'The Fourth, sir. Down the bottom of Number One Hold.'

'Oh, very well, very well! You stay here and see my gear aboard. As I'm obliged to conduct myself to my quarters, I shall do so.'

'Sure you can find the way, sir?'

'To the sailor all ships are the same, Quartermaster,' Ebbs told him solemnly. 'They float on the water, they contain machinery, they feed you and sleep you. It is only the people inside them who differ. Kindly remember that.'

He strode off forward, gripping his trilby, his mackintosh flapping violently round his legs in the cold wind lightly loaded with snow that was blowing off the Estuary.

The *Charlemagne*, which was known to all British seafarers as the Charley Mange, was one of the smaller Pole Star Liners. She was designed for six hundred passengers in the modern tradition of painstakingly flouting as many of the conventions of naval architecture as possible. Nothing could be done to the shape of her hull, for the *Cutty Sark's* has yet to be bettered; but the funnels that in the 'thirties numerically indicated a ship's vigour were swept into one truncated stack, the weary ventilators were cleared from her decks, and the masts reduced to a single spike above the bridge. Her first-class saloons repeated the modern idiom by assuming the ocean to be something shameful, to be hidden away from the passengers as much as possible, and had been decorated by an amiable young man who was hairy with tweed and rough with corduroy and had been no further to sea than the balcony of *The Prospect of Whitby*. She also offered tourist-class accommodation, found at the bottom of a narrow companionway leading towards the stern. The descent of these stairs had the same discouraging effect on a passenger seeking his cabin as a climb to the gallery in a London theatre: the pastel shades gradually hardened, the springy decking underfoot turned into ringing linoleum, the lights stared disagreeably through thick plain glass, and the sea breezes carefully directed by the designers into the first class staterooms were replaced by the alternate smells of hot oil from the engine-room and hot fat from the galley.

Ebbs distributed glares at the cigarette packets, scraps of newspaper, spent matches, and empty beer bottles scattered everywhere by the dockers, giving the decks the look of a football stand on a Saturday night. He had a sharp eye for untidiness beyond the blind spot of himself, and was already composing orders for cleaning up his ship when he reached the door labelled with brass dignity CAPTAIN.

He crossed the storm-step, and looked round his new apartments. In the *Martin Luther* he had occupied a green-painted steel nook between the gyro compass and the officers' oilskin locker, but command of the *Charlemagne* awarded him a day-cabin that was agreeably lined with polished wood and deep carpet, and would have comfortably accommodated the whole of his former crew. Remembering he was stepping into a sick man's home he abruptly took on an expression of reverence; but this dissolved as he stepped through to his night-cabin and found himself provided with a double bed under a pink silk counterpane. He bounced on this several times with satisfaction, then went into the bathroom and playfully tried all the taps. Returning to the day-cabin, he stood in the middle of the deck with his hands clasped behind him and jauntily inspected the furniture. The Company had designed the cabin firstly for the entertainment of passengers, making it resemble the tea lounge of a residential hotel. Apart from a desk the size of McWhirrey's, there were two pink sofas, several pink-and-gold easy chairs and matching tables, some pink-shaded lamps, three clocks with pink faces, pink-flowered curtains on the scuttles, pink-framed pictures on the bulkheads, and an open hearth in which a pair of incombustible logs smouldered in a permanent pink electric glow. In one corner was a pink-and-gold cabinet Ebbs took for a wardrobe, which he opened and found full of glasses, bottles, and cocktail shakers. He suddenly began to laugh: after his daily wrestle for comfort with the *Martin Luther* this crowning luxury glittered with ridicule.

He heard a cough behind him.

'Ah, Purser!' Ebbs recognised the white bands on his visitor's cuff.

'Good morning, sir. My name is Prittlewell. Herbert Prittlewell. I hope the cabin is satisfactory?'

'Perfectly, thank you.'

'I had your predecessor's gear removed as soon as I heard of his indisposition, sir.'

'Very sad, very sad,' Ebbs said, becoming solemn again. 'I have – ah, of course, sent some flowers and grapes and so forth.'

'I'm sure you have, sir.'

Prittlewell looked at Ebbs shrewdly. As the *Charlemagne's* hotel manager he spent his life assessing people, separating the ones who were genuinely important, wealthy, honest, or married from those taking advantage of the isolation of the sea to pretend they were. He was a tall grey handsome man with a monocle, like a cartoon Admiral, and he had a graceful manner that might have flowered first in Dartmouth, an older public school, or at least South Kensington. But Prittlewell had been to none of these places. He had begun as a fourteen-year-old bell-boy aboard a Pole Star liner, where he found that packages of soap, butter, tea, and cutlery could be safely smuggled ashore in a gutted copy of a Mission Bible and sold handsomely to the neighbours in his native Stepney. This spirit had quickly projected him through the lower ranks of stewards, but he soon became dissatisfied with such trivial scrounging and set himself to acquire book-keeping, good manners, and a wardroom accent, in order to achieve control of the dozen silent percentages and score of unmentioned favours that bring power and profit to the purser of a large liner.

'I've brought your own gear up, sir,' he said, as two stewards struggled in with the loaf-shaped leather trunk and dozen paper parcels in which Ebbs moved his possessions.

'Thank you, Purser.'

'This is your first command of a passenger ship, I believe, sir?' Prittlewell had speculated more sharply than anyone on board about Ebbs' accession to the *Charlemagne*, as his income depended largely on keeping the Captain's eyes from his account books.

'I really can't see why that is of any importance,' Ebbs told him. 'To the sailor all ships are the same. They float on the water, they contain machinery, they feed you and sleep you. It is only the people inside them who matter. I should like you to remember that, please.'

'Certainly, sir.'

Ebbs sat down in his pink desk chair. 'I gather we have a full ship for the voyage?'

'Yes, sir. Not a spare shed.'

'I beg your pardon?'

'No unoccupied cabins, sir. Perhaps you would like to see the passenger list?'

'Ah, thank you!' Ebbs eagerly took a bundle of typewritten flimsy. 'Nothing like starting work at once, eh? Well, well!' he murmured, flicking over the smudgy sheets. 'Remarkable, isn't it? Here are these people, whom I couldn't tell from Adam and Eve, and by the end of the voyage we'll all be firm friends and know each other inside out.'

'Most remarkable, sir.'

'If you will kindly give me half an hour,' Ebbs went on, 'I shall prepare a list of people I wish to sit at my table. A somewhat chancy selection, I think? Like picking horses. However, from the ages and occupations so thoughtfully provided by the head office, I should be able to gather some congenial company. I don't want any young women – '

'The Company have already sent me a list of passengers who will be sitting at your table, sir.'

'You mean I have no say in the matter at all?'

'None whatever, sir.'

He handed Ebbs another flimsy.

'But – but supposing I don't like these persons?'

'I'm sorry, but there's nothing you can do about it. You could take your meals in your cabin, I suppose, sir. But that would hardly recommend itself to the Company.'

'No, of course not.' Ebbs frowned. 'It's very inconsiderate.'

'You appreciate, sir, a seat at your table is an honour which carries a substantial social position on board?'

'Anyway, I shall have my breakfast in my cabin at sea,' Ebbs said decisively, tossing the papers on his desk. 'Breakfast is not a sociable meal. What's that?'

'The list of guests who will be attending your cocktail party, sir.'

'I appear to be in the position, Purser, of a child having its first birthday treat?'

Prittlewell's shoulders hesitated on a shrug. 'It's the custom of the Line, sir.'

Ebbs was beginning to feel uneasy. The *Martin Luther's* catering had been managed by a beery Irishman with dirty finger-nails who obediently shuffled the few dishes on the menu at his command, but Prittlewell affected him like an undertipped head waiter.

'I don't suppose there's anyone in particular travelling with us, is there?' he asked, his good spirits evaporated. 'No – ah, celebrities?'

'There are six parsons, sir.'

'Six!' Ebbs was shocked. 'I'm not a superstitious man, Purser, but that augurs badly.'

'I agree, sir. One dog-collar is usually considered sufficient to blight a voyage. I was with Captain Graham in the *Hannibal* when he dropped dead in the middle of the fancy-dress dance. A party of missionaries we were bringing back from Singapore was generally held responsible. And there were only four of them.'

'Let us sincerely hope these will prove less murderous,' Ebbs said sombrely. Prittlewell gathered the interview was at an end. 'I will hold a conference of officers tomorrow,' Ebbs added. 'Is there any sign of the Chief Officer?'

'Not on board yet, sir.'

'Not yet? But I sent the fellow an extremely urgent telegram. I'll have to wire again, that's all. What do you suppose could have happened to him?'

Prittlewell looked thoughtful. 'He may have been detained, sir,' he suggested.

'Detained? But how? Where?'

'The Chief Officer has many friends who press their hospitality in London,' Prittlewell told him. He thought that a reasonably honest reply.

3

John Reginald Ernest Maitland Wilson Shawe-Wilson, RNR, Chief Officer of the *Charlemagne*, mounted the gangway early the next morning suffering from a bad hangover, lack of sleep, and surfeit of affection, his usual condition when returning from leave. He was also in a black temper. He had taken Ebbs' appointment as a personal insult. He would concede that youth prevented the Pole Star Line from offering command of the *Charlemagne* to himself, but to place above him the skipper of a seedy tramp, a roughneck navigator, an ocean guttersnipe, was too much. And now the man was harrying him with telegrams, robbing him of his just leave, and curtailing the warm exploration of his last voyage's romance with an active girl whom he had barely an hour before regretfully left in bed.

'The Captain wants to see you immediate, sir,' said the Quartermaster, saluting.

'He'll have to wait till I've changed. Get this bag taken to my cabin.' He dropped his suitcase on the deck.

Shawe-Wilson's cabin, unusually tidy through his absence, was a smaller and more nautical apartment than Ebbs', for the only entertaining of passengers therein was clandestine and usually conducted with the light out. The severe paint, brass, and woodwork was everywhere brightened by covers, cloths, and cushions presented to him at the end of voyages damp with the tears of their donors, half a dozen of whom looked yearningly from the locker in which he rummaged for his aspirin. He glanced warily in the bulkhead mirror and saw that the face that had fluttered a thousand hearts on the boat-deck was paled and shadowed. He rang for tea and began his toilet. He showered, brushed his teeth with chlorophyll paste, rinsed his mouth with Listerine, shaved, massaged his cheeks with Eau de Cologne, dabbed deodorant under his arms, puffed talc between his toes, and sprinkled brilliantine on his hair; every morning he took himself as a French chef accepts a raw lettuce, to be suitably oiled and dressed before presentation to the public. Scattering his shore-going clothes on the deck, he selected his best doeskin uniform, fresh from Gieves, drew shirt, collar, tie, socks, and handkerchiefs from monogrammed leather cases, dressed himself thoughtfully, then stepped from the cabin to face again his responsibilities.

It was not yet eight o'clock, and bacon and eggs were ready for *Charlemagne's* officers among the stacked chairs and rolled carpets of the first-class dining saloon. He found Ebbs, who like all clean-living men fondly relished his breakfast, sitting at the head of the long table alone.

'Mr Wilson, isn't it?' Ebbs asked, extending his arm cordially across the cloth.

'Shawe-Wilson. How do you do, sir.'

'I should have preferred to make your acquaintance earlier,' said Ebbs, feeling he must make a show of Captain's disapproval and anxious to get it over. 'I sent you two telegrams, both urgently requesting your return from leave.'

Shawe-Wilson sat down and reached for the coffee. 'I didn't get either of them till this morning,' he explained airily. 'I've been away in the country with the Purcells. Do you know the Purcells, sir?'

'No, Mr Shawe-Wilson. I do not shoot.'

'Your first command of a passenger ship, I hear?' the Chief Officer continued.

'That is not of the slightest importance, Mr Shawe-Wilson,' Ebbs said, becoming irritated. 'To the sailor all ships are the same. They float on the water, they contain machinery, they feed you and they put you up. Only the people inside them matter. Kindly bear that in mind.'

'Of course, sir. Pass the sugar, will you?'

Ebbs blew his nose. He had no wish to start the voyage by an open row with his chief executive, but he wondered where he had ever come across such an objectionable young man.

'After breakfast,' Ebbs said firmly, 'I should be obliged if you would conduct me round the ship. Unless, of course, you have other social engagements?'

'Chart pencils,' Ebbs declared, as they stood alone shortly afterwards in the cold chartroom. 'Where are the chartroom pencils, Mr Shawe-Wilson?'

'Generally stolen in port, sir,' Shawe-Wilson said wearily.

'Then you must see others are provided immediately. Chartroom pencils are navigational equipment, and navigational equipment is the responsibility of the Chief Officer. It is stated quite clearly in the Company Regulations. What happens if there aren't any chart pencils? Why, we take an important bearing leaving port and by the time we've marked it on the chart we're aground. You may possibly consider me fussy, Mr Shawe-Wilson – it is a charge that I suppose might be made behind my back – but the efficient running of the ship depends on everyone being able to put their hands on things exactly as they want them.'

'Yes, sir.'

'Right, Mr Shawe-Wilson. Let us proceed. What else have we up here?'

'I suppose you want to see the accommodation for passenger's pets, sir?'

'I want to see everything. Lead the way, please.'

Ebbs summoned the officers' conference the following afternoon at five, an hour when the sailor's attention in port drifts towards the gangway and the sweet inevitability of opening-time.

The change of command made no difference to most of the crew, to whom the Captain was as remote as God and as comfortably discountable in the arrangements of daily life, but to the men who lived next to him and could hear him singing in his bath he achieved a personal importance inconceivable to any landsman. Nelson had hardly been missed more sorrowfully by his shipmates than the easy-going Captain Buckle; and now this Ebbs had been sprung on them, unknown and unpredictably full of new notions, and they had to adapt themselves to him with the good grace of comfortable Civil Servants facing a violent change in government.

'Well, gentlemen, may I introduce myself?' Ebbs began jovially, anxious to start aright with the dozen or so men who gathered in the empty first-class smoke-room. 'I must say I should have appreciated a more active welcome on my arrival. But one must draw a moral, gentlemen – it has probably forestalled any feelings I might have of self-importance. We shall now say no more about it. My appointment to this vessel came as something of a shock – a sad shock, naturally, gentlemen – but with your co-operation I trust it will be a success. I am sure I can rely on you all for that.'

He beamed round the audience, who were inspecting him anxiously. 'No doubt before we sail my former crew will tell you – ah, all you wish to know about me,' Ebbs continued brightly. 'It's just that I have certain ways of doing things, and I shall be glad if you will do me the courtesy of observing them. I don't believe it's that I'm fussy, gentlemen. Not at all. I'm sure I do not deserve the' – he blew his nose – 'age and femininity I have occasionally heard ascribed to me by junior officers. As long as you stick to Company Regulations, gentlemen, you will find me a perfectly fair and understanding Captain.'

As each of his listeners had wormed a comfortable hole for themselves somewhere in the Company's laws for the conduct of its ships and its officers, they now began to exchange glances of alarm.

'I would particularly like to mention the subject of drinking,' Ebbs said. Half their faces fell. 'I am perfectly broad-minded, gentlemen, and realise the importance of an occasional drink as a stimulant. But after my years at sea I can safely say that I prefer on most occasions a good clean glass of water from the tap. I hope, gentlemen, I shall observe no drunkenness while at sea. The other point concerns mixing with passengers. Particularly female passengers.' The faces of the other half sagged. 'I hope my junior officers will abide by Company Regulations and stay clear of the passenger decks. To the true sailor passengers are merely animated cargo. However,' he went on, resuming his former cheerfulness and earnestly hoping he was making a good impression, 'I'm sure we shall have a happy voyage. This ship, which I see bears the proud name of an Emperor of the Goths – '

'Wasn't it the Franks, sir?' asked Brickwood, a plump young man, the Second Mate.

'Goths,' Ebbs said. 'I have naturally studied the names of all the ships in the Company's fleet. Emperor of the Goths, who lived some eight hundred years B.C. – '

'Wasn't it A.D., sir?' Brickwood asked.

'Mr Brickwood, I really must ask you to let me make my point. I happen to have read the Company's history with great care.'

'I beg your pardon, sir.'

'That is perfectly all right, Mr Brickwood. But to proceed – '

'I felt you might have made a slip of the tongue, sir.'

'Well, I haven't. To proceed – ' Ebbs caught sight of a large painting above Brickwood's head, of a man with high blood-pressure and yellow whiskers, entitled *Charlemagne, Emperor of the Franks, 742-814 A.D.* He blew his nose again. 'Well, anyway, all ships are the same to the seafarer,' he went on. 'They float on the water, contain machinery, feed you and sleep you. Only the people in them matter. Remember that, gentlemen. Any questions?'

But the only points on which Ebbs had roused their curiosity were unmentionable in his hearing.

Ebbs usually spent his leave in a small house in Acton with his elder sister, a powerful woman who believed he was in a state of suspended adolescence, and before every voyage filled him with advice on the importance of washing his neck, changing his socks, closing his pores, and opening his bowels. His home life had been spread so thinly over his years afloat that he was now no more than a disturbing visitor to her house, whose memory was conscientiously kept afresh by the litter of souvenirs the sea had swept into the parlour, and the row of photographs on the mantelpiece which showed him gradually gaining rank and losing hair in the Company's service. As Ebbs had no friends ashore and no interests outside his ship, he passed his few days in port energetically crawling round the *Charlemagne* from the cramped radar cabin high on her monkey island to the pipes packed like spaghetti in a box down in the duck keel. Whenever he returned to his cabin he found the desk piled more thickly with letters from the office and fierce memoranda from McWhirrey, most of which he was unable to understand. The rest of his time was occupied by the tailors' urgently fitting him for mess jackets and by listening to the Company's Marine Superintendent, who settled himself every morning in his best armchair

17

with a fresh bottle of whisky and offered progressively pointless advice.

With a blast of alarm Ebbs realised three mornings later that within twenty-four hours his ship was due to sail. The accumulated injuries of her last voyage were still being repaired by grimy men with welding-torches and blow-lamps who sliced steel fixtures from the decks, skinned the paintwork, and dragged pieces of machinery through the saloons, giving her the appearance of already being in the hands of the ship-breakers. The alleyways were still carpeted with oily canvas and choked with piles of mattresses, the cabin furniture was crammed into the bunks, the saloons were featureless under dust sheets, and it seemed to him that the ship would never be ready to receive the delicate mariners of her passengers list at all. But somehow the *Charlemagne* made herself ready for sea. Suddenly the decks were cleaned, set, and lit like a stage, the ruffians with reeking pails in the alleyways were turned into neatly white-jacketed urbane Pole Star stewards, and flowers came aboard by the armful and telegrams in orange sheaves to illuminate the gloom of departure. The ship fell into the unusual silence that claimed her only immediately before and after every voyage, between the hammering of the repairers and the chatter of passengers. And in the evening Sir Angus came aboard, an Admiral in a bowler hat, to make his inspection.

'You seem to have familiarised yourself with the vessel very well,' he conceded, as he walked with Ebbs along the deck afterwards.

Ebb blew his nose in relief. 'You appreciate, I hope, Captain, that this command will be somewhat different than your last?'

'I have always held, Sir Angus, that all ships are the same from the sailors' point of view. They float on the water, they – '

'Possibly. Seamanship is naturally the first consideration, but the passengers don't think twice about their safety these days – no more than you or I about the earth going round the sun. It's the size of their cabins and the size of their breakfasts that matter to them. The daily life on board.'

'The – ah, fun and games?' Ebbs suggested.

'The trouble is, we're now facing real competition for passenger traffic. Look at that,' he continued bitterly, pulling a folded magazine from his overcoat pocket. Ebbs inspected a coloured advertisement showing the soft-lined interior of an aeroplane, in which tall men in crisp suits and chic bewitching women sipped steady Martinis and chatted in a joyous intimacy appropriate to the Heavens. 'Glamorised bloody aeroplanes!' McWhirrey scowled. 'We have to play their game, that's all. Fortunately we hold a few of the cards. Sunshine, moonlight…good food, cheap drinks…adventure, excitement, romance,' he went on, as if mouthing the words of a foreign language. 'Our aim must be to make every voyage a holiday. You understand, Captain?'

'I shall certainly foster the holiday spirit, Sir Angus,' Ebbs told him earnestly.

'Each of our ships must provide a courtship for the young, a second honeymoon for the middle-aged, and a rejuvenation for the elderly.'

'I'll do my best, sir,' he said more doubtfully.

'You're not married, are you?'

'Still single, sir.'

'Then I'll remind you that the margin between a Captain's social duties and impropriety may sometimes be dangerously narrow.' McWhirrey looked at him closely. 'Drink and women, you know.'

'I assure you, sir,' Ebbs said hastily, 'I am most abstemious… '

'In a ship like this, where the bar's open twelve hours a day?'

'And as for the other, Sir Angus… ' He smiled away the ridiculous.

'It may pay you to remember that the sea sometimes has a peculiar effect on women travelling alone,' said McWhirrey weightily. 'Like gin.'

They reached the door of Ebbs' cabin. McWhirrey stopped. 'You are in charge of a vessel containing a thousand lives and costing near on three million pounds. Do you feel absolutely confident to handle her in all circumstances? If not, now is the time to say so.'

'Perfectly confident, sir!'

Sir Angus nodded. 'Very well. I will be satisfied with that. By the way, you'll have to squeeze in an extra passenger. Fellow called Broster – Brigadier Broster. A big shareholder in the Line and an old personal friend of mine, as a matter of fact. A very decent chap. Just treat him as you would any other member of the passenger list – that's all he expects.'

'Broster? I'll remember that, Sir Angus.'

'Now how about a glass of whisky? It's a cold night.'

4

When the *Charlemagne's* passengers had booked their berths in the elegant Pole Star passenger office in Cockspur Street, the voyage had the excitement of the distant battle of new recruits. But the weeks slipped surprisingly away, until they suddenly found themselves nibbling their breakfast with the faint appetite of departing voyagers, and wondering where the devil the passports had got to and how they could finish the packing. Their last morning fled treacherously: too soon came the alarming peal of the door-bell and the impatient peak-capped man on the mat. Jumping on their stubborn cases, collecting their children in a flurry of smackings, leaving a hundred things unpacked and unsaid, they started in panic for the station. Gathering under the smoky glass arch, horrified at the sight of their irrevocable companions for the next four weeks, they waited pathetically in the bitter wind blowing down the rails as their luggage and children kept perversely disappearing into the crowd, while porters with electric trolleys drove sportively through them like tanks among demoralised infantry. The boat trains dragged them through the sulphurous tunnels and round the soot-pickled tenements of the East End, and left them at Tilbury to be barked into pens by officials and bent beneath the humiliating governmental rites of departure. At last they were allowed to cross the moat of muddy Thames water to their ship under the farewell glances of policemen, searching hopelessly in their pockets for the tickets by which the Pole Star Line undertook to transport them to Australia, specifically refusing responsibility for their loss *en route* by storm, fire, shipwreck, stranding, thunderbolt, strike, mutiny, revolution, war, plague, or pirates.

The decks rang with Sirs and Madams as their baggage was snatched by the stewards, who were already accurately calculating the size of their eventual tips. Prittlewell stood bowing by the first-class gangway, suavely deflecting the earliest questions and complaints; the ship's officers leant eagerly from the boat deck, assessing every girl coming aboard through the bridge glasses; and Shawe-Wilson strode through the incoming passengers with his cap at a Beatty angle, issuing curt commands to surprised sailors whenever he sensed a sufficient audience of young women.

The only man idle in the animated ship was Ebbs. As nobody seemed to want him and he could think of no one to summon, he was alone in his pink cabin sitting uncomfortably on his sharp anticipations. He was not an imaginative man, but as he looked through the scuttles at the thickening snow that would shortly be falling on his own exposed shoulders he could clearly see at least a dozen ingenious disasters that might shortly overtake the *Charlemagne*.

The ship sailed with four tugs pulling her into the truculent wind like puppies biting on their leads, while the BBC announcer, warm and dry in his studio, cosily forecast imminent severe gales in Dover, Wight, Portland, and Plymouth, right across her path. From the first salvo of breaking glasses as she started pitching in the short-tempered Channel seas, the passengers began to reel and falter under the weather's attack. They lay miserably gripping the rails of their lively bunks as the ship steamed unhappily through the night away from England, and the next morning only a few insensitive travellers appeared on the rainy decks, calling bravely to each other 'It'll be worse in the Bay!' Then she turned south round Ushant and crossed the bellicose Atlantic rollers on their way to pound the coast of France, and even these hearties groaned in their cabins or stared torpidly at the blue-and-gold cards stuck over every wash-basin saying, *The Captain, Officers, and Crew of R.M.S. 'Charlemagne' Wish You a Most Pleasant Voyage.*

The ship reduced speed as crockery fell like September fruit and the legs of men and furniture stood in jeopardy; then she jumped and quivered in the waves all down the long Iberian coast from Cape Finisterre to St Vincent. The crew had never known such weather, even old hands who held that modern gales, like modern beers, had nothing of their former manly strength. By cheerful shipboard superstition the blame for their misfortune had to be laid on someone, and although a few hands accused the six parsons who now rolled feebly in their bunks below, to most of the crew the Jonah who had attracted the spiteful Heavens was clearly Ebbs.

The *Charlemagne* reached Gibraltar before the weather changed. The wind and sea dropped away from her in exhaustion, the sun rose in shameless splendour, and she sailed past the Rock into a day of spacious blue sky punctured by fast neat white clouds. A warm breeze swept through the freshly-opened scuttles and blew away the smell of vomit, the decks began to steam and dry in the sun, and the passengers rose like a graveyard at the Resurrection.

That morning Ebbs came jauntily into his cabin from the bridge, throwing his damp greatcoat on to a pink sofa.

'A welcome smell!' he said, rubbing his hands.

'Good morning, sir,' said Albert Burtweed, the Captain's Tiger. 'Your breakfast.' He uncovered a silver dish on the freshly-docile table, as though presenting the plate in church. 'Kidneys, bacon and chop, sir.'

The Tiger was a thin, neat man, with oval gold-rimmed spectacles, a bald head ringed with white fluff, and a bad case of widely divaricating toes known among ocean stewards as 'Cunard Feet.' Without his white Pole Star jacket he had the pleasantly diffident appearance of a pensionable clerk or an undernourished clergyman; but he was a true sailor who distrusted paving-stones, and had penetrated the five continents no further than the first bar by the dock where he could buy a glass of beer and talk tenderly of England. Burtweed had neither roof nor relatives ashore and lived continuously in his ship, spending his forced spells of separation during fumigation and overhaul in the chilly galleries of the Sailors' Home. He was an instinctive servant, of the type now forgotten on land and becoming rare even at sea, who for more than forty years had skilfully balanced trays down Pole Star alleyways and could never serve a soup-plate without dignity nor fold a handkerchief short of perfection.

'An inauspicious start to the voyage, sir,' Burtweed said, spreading a napkin over his master's lap as he sat down. He had not yet had a chance to assess Ebbs, but he already looked on him as 'His Captain' in the way a farmhand regards a bull or pig entrusted for feeding and cleaning to his care, and he was determined to make him a prizewinner.

'Not entirely, Burtweed,' Ebbs said cheerfully. 'We must draw a moral. I have experienced handling the ship in the worst possible weather, and although it's been something of a strain I know I have nothing more to fear in that direction. I can start turning my energies to more social duties.'

'Are you partaking luncheon in the saloon, sir?'

Ebbs swallowed a mouthful of kidney, and shook his head. So far he had eaten his meals on the bridge, and had hardly penetrated further into the ship than his cabin. 'As I haven't had my clothes off since leaving London I feel entitled to turn in for the morning. Kindly bring me a pot of tea and some bread and jam about two.'

'Yes, sir. And dinner, sir?'

'I fancy I shall be strong enough to face the passengers by then. I only hope they will have equal fortitude.'

'Very good, sir.' Burtweed glanced modestly at Ebbs' meagre belongings, spread thinly over the cabin. There was a pokerwork pipe-rack, a photograph in a fretwork frame of his cadet group, a tobacco-jar like a decapitated Toby jug, a rope mat woven on his first voyage, a paperweight shaped like a modest mermaid, a free-gift set of Dickens between a couple of owls, a small unidentifiable object inscribed *Un Cadeau de Cherbourg*, a coloured picture of Windsor Castle, an inkstand suspended in a horseshoe, and a calendar that told the date for a hundred years either way.

'The arrangements are satisfactory, sir?' he asked.

'Perfectly satisfactory, thank you, Burtweed. Though I must confess to feeling somewhat lost in these apartments. I suppose Captain Buckle got used to them in time?'

'The poor gentleman's hobby took up a good deal of room, sir,' Burtweed said sadly, picking up Ebbs' greatcoat. 'He spent most of the time at sea making bits of furniture. Though with respect to him, sir, it's a relief to get rid of all them chips and shavings.'

'I have no hobbies, Burtweed,' Ebbs told him solemnly, cutting into his chop. 'Only my ship.'

'Very laudable, sir.'

There was a knock on the jalousie door and Prittlewell entered, tucking his cap under his left arm with a flourish.

'Good morning, Purser! How are the passengers?'

'As hungry as savages, sir.'

'Excellent, excellent! And what can I do for you?'

'I have a list of your social engagements during the voyage, sir.'

Ebbs' cheerfulness diminished.

'Not only my meals and my guests but my life is to be arranged for me?'

'It's the custom, sir.'

Ebbs glanced through the long dated list as he buttered a piece of toast. 'Sports Committee, Bathing Beauty Competition, Deck Cricket, Debating Society, Old Tyme Dancing, Horse Riding, Treasure Hunt, Divine Service, Bingo… Is my presence strictly necessary at all of these?'

'The passengers expect it, I'm afraid, sir.'

'But what about this – Children's Tea Party. What possible use can I be at a function like that? That's going a bit far, I must say.'

'I think I should tell you that Lady McWhirrey in London makes a particular point of the Captain being present, sir. And here is a plan of your table in the saloon.'

Ebbs took a card on which was typed:

Miss Annette Porter-Williams

Mr Dancer	Mrs Judd
Mrs William Coke	Mr William Coke
Canon Swingle	Mrs Lomax
Mrs Porteous	Mr Willy Boast

THE CAPTAIN

'Do you know anything about these people, Purser?' Ebbs asked hopefully. 'Any tittle-tattle that might help to make conversation?'

'I've seen most of them in my time,' Prittlewell said, as if discussing a music-hall bill. 'The Cokes are Australian millionaires – hearts of gold, but rather vulgar. Wool, you know. Old Mrs Lomax is travelling for her health. Boast writes books about cricket – '

'Does he, indeed? I admit I spend my life a thousand miles from the nearest blade of grass, but I know enough of the game to make a reliable source of conversation out of him, at least.'

'I doubt it, sir. He's been drunk since we left Tilbury. And the rest have been seasick.'

Ebbs' face fell. 'Dinner may be something of a trial tonight then, I fear?'

'Oh, undoubtedly, sir. Captain Buckle always said he'd gladly give a month's pay to get out of the first dinner at sea. And I have a note for you, sir.' He handed Ebbs an envelope marked PRIVATE AND CONFIDENTIAL. 'It's from Brigadier Broster.'

Ebbs opened the letter and read:

Dear Captain

I have never been so grossly insulted in my life. I altered my arrangements at the last moment specially to travel in this ship, at great personal inconvenience, and I have been put for my meals at a draughty table by the door (I suffer severely from lumbago) miles away from the galley so the food arrives stone cold, next to a ventilator swamping me with the smell of the engine-room, and in the exclusive company of five clergymen. I am not complaining. I may be a large shareholder in this Line and a personal friend of our Chairman, but I want to be treated exactly like any other passenger. Fair's fair. But on other Pole Star ships (not to mention Orient and P & O) I am at least offered a place at the Captain's table. Please take what action you think fit.

I have the honour to be, etc.,

Roger Broster

Ebbs gasped. 'But I've never received a letter like this in my life!' He blew his nose agitatedly. 'He seems a very difficult customer, Purser.'

'Renowned for it in the Line, sir. It was him who got Captain Isleworth chucked out of the *Maximillian.*'

'Oh, did he?' Ebbs asked blackly. 'Perhaps we'd better put him at my table, then. We could turn out this Canon fellow. Stick him with the other reverend gentlemen. They'll have a lot to talk about.'

'As you wish, sir.'

'That will be all,' Ebbs said, feeling he had heard enough.

'Very good, sir. We shall expect you for dinner.'

'Burtweed,' Ebbs said when Prittlewell had left. He had been staring for some minutes at the uncommunicative names of his guests.

'Sir?'

'You have been Tiger to a good many Captains, I believe?'

Burtweed smiled benevolently. 'Twenty-four, sir. And as nice a bunch of gentlemen as you could expect to meet,' he continued modestly, as if talking of his own successful children.

'Quite. I'll admit that I'm becoming a little uneasy about entertaining for dinner tonight nine complete strangers, one of whom has already sent me an extremely offensive letter.'

'It takes all sorts to make a passenger list, sir,' said Burtweed generously, starting to clear away the dishes.

'I wondered if you had any – ah, advice, any experience of former Captains to draw upon, as it were?' Ebbs asked him. 'What did Captain Buckle say to the passengers, for instance? Surely he had some sort of small talk up his sleeve?'

'I am proper glad you asked, sir,' Burtweed said with feeling. 'Really – I am, sir. Very difficult it can be sometimes at table, and I – I – ' He stared at his feet and swallowed. 'I *do* want you to be a success, sir. Not being able to offer advice unasked – '

'You are asked, Burtweed, you are asked.'

'Thank you, sir. Well, sir. The first thing, you must tell a funny story.'

Ebbs rubbed his chin. 'I don't think I know any funny stories.'

'Captain Buckle only had one, sir. He told it every voyage.'

'You remember it, Burtweed?'

'Bless us, yes sir! Fifty times I must have heard it, regular twice a voyage. It was a real scream, sir.'

'Perhaps you could repeat it to me?'

'With the greatest of pleasure, sir. It was about a Captain and a Chief Engineer – '

'Perfectly proper, I hope?' Ebbs asked severely.

'Oh, perfectly, sir! Never bring a blush to a cheek, Captain Buckle wouldn't. You see, this Captain, sir, was – with great respect – one of the old school, sir, and always heaved the lead when his ship was coming into port, like in the old days before echo-sounders and all that, sir. Well, this Captain prided himself he could tell what port they was in just by looking at the lead, sir, and seeing the mud what was brought up from the sea bottom. But one day the Chief Engineer grabs the lead, sir, on its way to the bridge, takes it to his cabin, and wipes his best boots in it. The Captain takes one look at it, you see, sir, and says to the mates: "Gentlemen," he says, "I have the honour to inform you that the ship is now situated at the corner of Sauchiehall Street and Argyll Street."'

There was silence.

'I see,' Ebbs said. He thought deeply, scratching his ear. 'Not a bad tale.'

'Had the passengers in fits sometimes, sir. Captain Buckle called it his ice-breaker.'

'It might possibly be not unamusing if told skilfully,' Ebbs decided. As a junior officer he had been tolerated as a shipboard raconteur, though he felt his skill had withered in the solitude of captaincy. 'I'll think it over, anyway,' he promised. He gave Burtweed a grateful nod. 'I intend to spare no pains to make tonight a success.'

5

The gentle Mediterranean, a longer civilised sea than the boisterous Atlantic, greeted the *Charlemagne* serenely with mild airs and charmed her through the day with courteous waves towards the North African coast. As the passengers' physiology was no longer strained by the weather they were able to exercise it vigorously in all directions: they ate heartily, slept soundly, walked the decks briskly, drank deeply, and made love lustily. The players skipped like early lambs on the deck-tennis courts, the girls pranced in premature swimsuits under the January sun, and all the young men pursued them round the decks unflaggingly.

At nightfall the ship became a gently-moving constellation, and the stewards' scales on the musical dressing-gongs signalled the start of a sportive shipboard evening. The passengers shook out their dress clothes and set the bell indicators flashing in the pantries like pin-tables, while in the first-class smoke-room Scottie the barman, his hair and smile carefully fixed, rattled a summoning tattoo with the leaping ice in his shaker. The passengers hastened to break their sickly abstinence, no longer the frozen bunch who had struggled thankfully up the gangway at Tilbury: they sat at ease in the well-advertised Pole Star luxury, ordering widening rounds of drinks and letting their personalities expand like sponges in the sea air.

A tall man with a white bristly moustache entered the smoke-room, paused at the door, assessed the company swiftly and without relish, and bowed towards a group sitting below a mural of three nude women floating on a blue sea like pink rubber ducks.

'Good evening!' he boomed, striding across. 'You will permit me to introduce myself? Name of Broster – Brigadier Broster. We're all at the Captain's table, I believe?'

He faced three people: a fat man with a complexion like a cut ham, a muscular blonde in a pink dress, and a pale pretty woman in black.

'It's a pleasure, Brigadier!' The fat man held out his hand. 'My name's Coke – Bill to you. I'm from Sydney. This is the sweetest little woman in the world – my wife Gwenny.'

'My now, isn't that nice?' said the blonde, shaking hands heartily.

'And our very pleasant shipboard friend, Mrs Judd.'

'Charmed, madam,' Broster said gruffly.

'Park yourself, Brigadier,' Bill Coke invited. 'Take a grog on us.'

'Not a bit, not a bit!' Broster assumed command of a chair. 'Much easier to leave it to me, I assure you. Steward!' The head smoke-room Steward hastened adroitly between the tables. 'Same stewards, I see, Mutt and Jeff,' Broster observed casually. 'Ah, Steward! Set up this round again, and tell Scottie to give me my usual.'

'Yes, sir! At once, sir! On behalf of the smoke-room hands, may I welcome you back, sir?'

'You certainly seem to know the ship well, Brigadier,' said Mrs Judd.

'Know it?' Broster laughed. 'Madam, I practically own it!'

They were impressed into silence.

'Steward!' Broster called, as soon as he tasted his drink.

'Sir?'

'Look here, Scottie can do better than that. Not a patch on his usual standard. Missed out the Cointreau altogether, I shouldn't be surprised. The proper way to make a White Lady,' he continued forcefully to his companions, 'is a couple of jiggers of gin, a jigger of lemon juice fresh from the fruit , and a whole jigger of Cointreau. That's how I've been taking it all my life, at any rate. In England,' he continued to the Cokes, as the Steward bore away the offending drink on a cloud of apologies, 'we often mix our own cocktails. We sometimes like to entertain our guests without servants in the room. We keep cellars in our houses – often very expensive cellars – and take great pride in them. Which reminds me of a very interesting story about cocktails. I recall I had some feller to dinner at my house – can't remember his name, but he was some MP or other – and told him I'd mix him any damn cocktail he'd care to mention. Any damn one. So he said he'd have a Chinese Dragon. And I *made* him a Chinese Dragon. After he'd drunk it he said, "Ah, but that wasn't a *real* Chinese Dragon. They're only made with arrack distilled in a particular place I happen to know in Hong Kong." So I showed him the bottle, and by George! It *was* genuine arrack, and it *did* come from that particular distillery. What do you think of that?'

Nobody said anything.

'Got to keep an eye on these people,' Broster went on, indicating the bar. 'Discipline's bound to be slack – new Captain, you know.'

'Why, we haven't seen the Captain yet, Bill?' Gwenny exclaimed, as if mentioning some interesting feature of the *Charlemagne's* structure.

'Aw, give him a chance, Gwenny,' her husband grunted. 'He was stuck on the bridge in that storm.'

'He's quite a young man, I believe?' Mrs Judd asked.

Gwenny giggled. 'And good looking?'

'I must remind you ladies,' Broster said, 'what sailors are?' He laughed heartily, and winked at Mrs Judd. 'That reminds me of a very interesting story about this ship – '

Ebbs was meanwhile declaring to his shaving mirror: 'There was once a Captain I sailed with as a cadet, who insisted on heaving the lead whenever he brought his ship into port. Just as he had been taught when he was a cadet himself. None of your scientific instruments on the bridge in those days, eh, ha ha! Ah, Burtweed,' he said, as the Tiger came into the bathroom carrying a silver tray. 'I've decided to tell this story of yours in the first person. It gives it more point.'

'Very true, I'm sure, sir.'

'What's that?' Ebbs asked.

'A large gin, sir. I thought you might need it.'

'I am not a drinking man, Burtweed, but I must say there are times when a stimulant is welcome.' He wiped the lather off his lips and swallowed the glassful. 'None of your scientific instruments on the bridge in those days,' he continued between razor-strokes. 'We sailed by our five senses and were proud of it. Now the Chief Engineer – and I'm sure,

Brigadier Broster, you will appreciate this point as a shipping man yourself – ' he digressed to the towel-rail – ' had taken a dislike to the Captain, and said – ' He paused, razor in mid-air. He thoughtfully wiped the lather on a towel. Should he make the Chief Engineer a Scot? 'And said, "Och aye, mon, ye canna tell wheer ye are wi' yon wee chunk o'lead – " Blast!' he exclaimed. He'd missed out the most important part, about the mud. 'Burtweed!' he called. 'Another gin, if you please.'

By the time Burtweed had helped him into the heavy stiff mess-jacket, bright with new gold braid, Ebbs was beginning to float pleasantly on an unaccustomed amount of alcohol.

'I look somewhat like a cigarette advertisement,' he said with unusual heartiness, eyeing himself in the long mirror. 'But I suppose the total effect is roughly what was intended. This bum-freezer fits all right?'

'Very tasteful, sir, I assure you.'

'Now, that story, Burtweed.' Ebbs pulled down his lapels decisively. 'I'm going to pad it out a bit – explain what the ship was doing, where she was going, why the Chief Engineer disliked the Captain, and so forth.'

'Captain Buckle sometimes made it last as long as four courses, sir.'

'I shall be glad enough if I can spread it over the soup. I don't know what the devil we shall talk about after that. The Lord will provide, I hope.'

'Yes, sir.'

'Are my trousers all right?'

'I could have done with a bit longer, sir.'

'Well, that was impossible. I must buy another pair in Sydney.'

From below came the faint chimes of the ship's gong: to Ebbs it sounded like the step of the executioner.

'My tie's straight?' he asked nervously.

'A treat, sir.'

'This is a big moment, Burtweed.' He ran his finger inside his stiff collar. 'A very big moment. Still, such things are sent to try us. As there's no point in delaying, I shall go down.'

Burtweed stopped him. 'Just one thing, sir.'

'Yes?'

'Your suspenders, sir.'

'What about them?'

'You have none on, sir.'

'I never wear them,' he said defiantly. After several squabbles with his sister, he still enjoyed the comfortable limpness of his socks.

'Oh, sir!' said Burtweed sorrowfully.

'But this is ridiculous! What a time to start talking about suspenders – are you out of your mind, man? Who on earth will know about it?'

Burtweed lowered his eyes. 'I shall know, sir.'

'Anyway,' Ebbs told him firmly. 'I haven't got any.'

'Will you wear mine, sir?' Burtweed pleaded. 'Just for tonight? Please, sir! It would make all the difference, I assure you, sir – ' He snatched up his trouser-legs, detached two greasy bands of mauve elastic from his skinny calves, and clipped them round Ebbs' submissive shanks. 'There, sir!' he said triumphantly. 'Now, sir, you are properly dressed all through.'

'At least I appreciate the thought,' Ebbs said grudgingly.

'Good luck, sir!' said Burtweed hoarsely. 'And don't worry, sir – *I* shall be there.'

There was a moment of illuminating sympathy between man and man, then Ebbs hurried away to dinner.

6

The first-class dining saloon in the *Charlemagne* fell agreeably on the senses: it was the Pole Star Line's biggest selling point. The tables glittered with lavish silver, the sideboards were hedged with gilt baskets of politely polished fruit, the stewards were waiting attentively in shining jackets, the band played mildly in the corner, and the cold buffet stretched the length of one bulkhead as brightly as a herbaceous border. Ebbs' stately table dominated the saloon from the far end, the Chief Engineer, Chief Officer, Purser, and Doctor each commanding a corner. They were the only representatives of the *Charlemagne's* crew in sight: her swarm of junior officers, who were strictly forbidden the passenger decks at all, dined separately in a mess-room far below in the unsophisticated atmosphere of enamel teapots and mustard pickles.

Immediately the gong sounded in the smoke-room, Broster rose and said: 'Must be getting in. After all, we at the Captain's table are expected to set something of an example. In England,' he explained to Bill Coke as though addressing an Aztec, 'we try to preserve some of the disappearing standards of behaviour. We generally go into dinner in pairs. I like to see these manners kept up in the Pole Star Line. In the first-class, of course. Madam —' He bowed to Mrs Judd. 'May I offer you my arm?'

'Delighted, Brigadier.'

'C'mon Gwenny,' Bill Coke said, sticking out his elbow. 'Hook on.'

By the time Ebbs reached the saloon door his table was already seated. He hesitated, pulled the Purser's card from his pocket, and set the names of the guests in his mind like a round robin. Then the glass doors were flung open by a pair of bowing stewards, and with a tweak at his tie he stalked resolutely through the chattering diners to his place.

He came to a stop at his chair.

'Good evening,' he said.

He looked quickly round the table. On his left he saw a honey-haired woman with bared shoulders; on his right, a man with thick spectacles and a floppy bow-tie, obviously drunk; between them, a frightening circle of unknown faces. And they saw a tall, worried, pleasant-looking man, with ruffled hair, a brand new mess-jacket, a crooked bow, and a pair of trousers that appeared to have been snatched urgently from the cleaners before reaching the presser.

'Good evening, Captain,' came raggedly from the table.

Ebbs sat down. He slowly picked up the stiffly-coned napkin in front of him, while his guests watched as if he were about to produce a pair of live rabbits from underneath.

'I wonder if you've heard the funny story…' he began. But at that moment everyone else said:

'Isn't it wonderful how calm the sea…?'

'Wasn't the sunset…?'

'Where have we got to in the…?'

'Can I pass the…?'

'Isn't it a real cow of…?'

They all paused, and looked at each other. Silence returned.

'Soup, sir?' Burtweed asked quickly.

'Thank you, Burtweed, soup.' Ebbs shook his handkerchief from his sleeve and wiped his forehead. The first course was served, and eaten like a funeral feast.

'Perhaps you've heard the funny story…' Ebbs began again, the determination of a lifetime at sea behind him.

'No, do go on!' the table exclaimed. They settled their eyes on him like schoolchildren with a new teacher.

'Well, it – it isn't hilariously funny really,' Ebbs mumbled, his nerve faltering.

'Please! Please go on, Captain!'

'Well, you see.' Ebbs swallowed. 'There was once an old Captain I knew, trained in the days of sail…one of the old sea-dogs, in fact.'

On his left, Mrs Porteous burst into uproarious giggles.

'One of the old sea-dogs,' Ebbs repeated warily, keeping his eye on her. 'Trained in the days of sail. When ships were propelled by – ah, sail.'

Seeing the funny point had not yet been reached, Mrs Porteous immediately silenced herself and followed his words with exaggerated attention.

'And whenever he took his ship into port, this Captain, he always had his Quartermaster standing by to heave the lead. In the old-fashioned way, you understand. You see, he was an old-fashioned Captain.'

'For whom the turbot?' demanded Burtweed.

As the second course was set on the table the cutlery tinkled in Ebbs' ear like dentists' instruments. He prayed that food might seduce the passengers' minds away from entertainment; but they returned to him with fearful politeness.

'Do go on, Captain! Yes, do tell us!' they insisted. 'We're dying to hear! Please, Captain! We're all listening!'

'Well,' Ebbs continued, warming up a little. 'He ordered the Quartermaster to heave the lead to see how much water there was under the ship…'

'How?' asked Bill Coke.

'I beg your pardon?'

'How did he see how much water there was under the ship?'

'Shhhhh, Billy!' his wife called across the table. 'Don't bitch up the Captain's story.'

'No, I'm interested, darling,' he said impatiently. 'Put me wise, will you, Captain? How did this lead show what water there was under the ship?'

'Well, you see…'

'Don't mind my asking, Captain, do you?'

'No, no, not at all,' Ebbs assured him. 'It's a very simple principle, really. The lead hits the bottom, and…and shows how deep it is.'

'Yes, but how's he get it up again?'

'It's on a line.'

'On a line! Now I get it.'

'You're a dumb cluck, Bill,' said his wife.

'Please go on with your story, Captain,' said Mrs Judd quickly.

'Well,' Ebbs persisted, 'this Captain had a boast. He claimed he could tell exactly where the ship was, in any part of the world, just by looking at the mud from the bottom of the sea, which sticks to the lead when it's brought up.'

The table, certain this was the climax, broke into amazed exclamations: 'No! Never! Really? Impossible!'

'Yes,' Ebbs continued grimly. 'Wherever the ship was – '

'Steward!' Brigadier Broster shouted across the saloon.

'Sir?'

'It is my fixed practice always to make my own salad dressing. As I have salad at every meal you had better get used to it now. I shall require some vinegar – tarragon vinegar. You have tarragon vinegar? Best olive oil, the white of an egg, a clove of garlic, a spring of parsley, borage, and chopped almonds. And I must have a silver dish to mix it in. Terribly important to take plenty of roughage at sea,' he continued to the table. 'No wonder there's so much constipation on ships. I've travelled round the world a couple of dozen times, and I think I can speak with some experience. In England, you know, we grow our own vegetables. We have large gardens attached to our houses, and employ several gardeners. I haven't put my teeth into a foreign vegetable for forty years. Not one! Just think of that. I should like to see everyone on board forced to take at least once a day a home-grown green salad, which contains vitamins A, B, C, and D, together with certain salts and minerals… '

Brigadier Broster trampled heavily over the conversation for several minutes, and as he paused to order chicken *en casserole* Ebbs said: 'But one day the Chief Engineer wiped his boots on it, and the Captain said, "Well, gentlemen, it seems the ship is at the corner of Sauchiehall Street and Argyll Street."'

There was immediate silence. Everyone looked at him in amazement.

'I didn't quite catch, Captain,' called old Mrs Lomax, shaking her hearing aid.

'It doesn't matter,' said Ebbs miserably. 'It was nothing.'

'Partaking entrée, sir?' Burtweed asked gently.

Shawe-Wilson had meanwhile outstripped Ebbs in conversation. As the saloon seating was arranged by the Purser and shipboard administration is largely a matter of reciprocal favours, he found himself drinking alone with five pretty girls.

'But what a lot of medals you've got,' said the blonde on his right.

'Oh, those.' He looked at his campaign ribbons as if noticing them for the first time. 'One more or less couldn't help picking up gongs in corvettes.'

'Corvettes!' the girls gasped, *The Cruel Sea* lapping sombrely at their memories.

'Yes, actually,' he said carelessly. He snapped his fingers. 'Steward! More chicken.' He was a hearty eater out of port.

The five girls regarded him with open admiration. His mess-jacket sat perfectly on his shoulders, his tie was geometrically precise, his shirt-front gleamed like porcelain, his teeth flashed, his cheeks shone, his hair emitted a reticent and manly tang. He had taken almost as long to prepare as the dinner.

'How terribly dangerous!' another girl breathed.

'Oh, it had its moments,' he admitted. 'But mostly it was frightfully boring. Oh, yes,' he said, laughing casually. 'One got used to sleeping on the bridge, living on biscuit and cocoa, the gales, the torpedoes, bombs, mines, and all that... It was simply the Battle of the Atlantic. The convoy had to get through. But the men, you know...the lives of every one of them in one's hands. Frightful responsibility.'

'Do tell us some of your experiences,' one of the girls implored, wide-eyed.

He awarded them all a smile. 'I'm sure you wouldn't be interested...'

'Oh, yes, we would!'

'Well, I wasn't in anything terribly spectacular except when we had a go at the *Bismarck*...'

The girls gasped.

'We were the first ship to stop her – one afternoon in an Atlantic gale. Almost immediately she opened fire. Rotten luck, first shot hit us right on the bridge. Fortunately I was blown clear, with nothing worse than a broken bone or two. Rest of the officers wiped out – steering wrecked – crew about to panic. Bit of luck, I recovered consciousness. I struggled aft to the emergency steering gear. "What are you going to do, sir?" the Cox'n

asked – he was rattled, poor fellow – "Why, attack and sink her, of course!"
I told him. He thought I was joking – a broadside from her could have
smashed us to iron filings. But I had a plan. Engine-room was intact, thank
God, so I worked round to windward and laid down smoke. It went rolling
ahead of us in the gale, and I was just going in to let her have it with our
torpedoes when the big ships went and finished her off.'

'Golly!' said the girls. Their food was cold and untouched in front of
them.

Shawe-Wilson helped himself to another glass of wine, provided by one
of the girls. For an instant he saw himself in command of a shattered
corvette, instead of Fourth Mate in a tired Pole Star tramp awaiting the
quietus of a torpedo.

'I certainly hope you had a rest after that,' an Australian girl said
reverently.

'As a matter of fact, the Doc told me to get out of corvettes,' he told
her, reaching for the menu. 'So I put in for a transfer. I spent the rest of
the war in mine disposal.'

On Ebbs' table conversation had died: they ate like ten strangers at a lunch
counter.

As he silently started his chicken Ebbs realised that his left suspender
was unhooked. He cursed Burtweed silently. He was now faced with an
overriding problem. If he left the suspender, it would trail after him when
he quitted the saloon as noticeably as a ball and chain; but to disappear
under the table to fasten it while he still sat under the passengers'
judgement was unthinkable.

After several minutes' unhappiness, Ebbs saw a brilliant compromise.
He would lean down stealthily and tuck the liberate elastic into his sock.

He glanced warily round the table. Everyone was eating as if
concentrating on a painful duty. He slowly let his left arm slip down his
leg and started groping round his shoe. He brushed clumsily against Mrs
Porteous' stocking. Immediately the pressure was firmly returned, and she
gave him a look signifying that an inviolable relationship had now been
established between them.

'You will come and have a liqueur with me after dinner, won't you?' she purred, laying a hand on his arm. 'Unless, of course, you'd prefer your rum?'

'I must get up to the bridge,' Ebbs muttered in panic. He snatched wildly for conversation. At the far end of the table Annette Porter-Williams and young Mr Dancer had spent the meal in an unconcerned intimate silence. 'Enjoying the trip?' Ebbs called heartily.

She looked up in surprise. She was a girl at the age when they all look pretty, and exactly the same.

'Perfectly beastly,' she said decisively.

Ebbs tried to smile. 'How do you like the ship?' he asked.

'Perfectly lovely,' she said. Annette had a small reservoir of conversation, and drained it drop by drop.

'Captain, you remind so much of a dear, dear friend,' Mrs Porteous murmured in his ear.

'Gibraltar!' Ebbs cried, being the first thing he could think of. 'Yes, Gibraltar!' He rubbed his hands together urgently. 'Who's been to Gibraltar?'

'I wish you'd put in there, Captain,' Bill Coke said cheerily: 'I've always wanted to see those monkeys on the Rock.'

'I can tell you something very interesting about the superstition concerning British rule and the apes on the Rock,' Brigadier Broster began immediately. 'It appears that the legend was originally fostered... '

'Aw, get along, Bill!' Gwenny Coke interrupted. 'You can see all the monkeys you want in Taronga Park zoo.'

'Yeah, but these monkeys are different monkeys, Gwenny.'

'Well, I can't see how any monkey's different from any other monkey.'

'Now see here, Gwenny,' her husband said crossly. 'Since when have you set yourself up as an authority on monkeys?'

'Ever since I married into your family, Bill Coke.'

He jumped to his feet. His chair fell back and crashed into the sweet trolley. 'I'll thank you not to insult my family in front of strangers!' he shouted.

'I suppose you can't take a joke any more?' Gwenny snapped.

'I don't call that much of a joke!'

'And I don't call that much of a sense of humour!'

'I'm going back to the bar – good night!' He banged the table violently, rattling the cutlery.

'And don't come back to the cabin slobbering over me when you're dead drunk!' she screamed.

Willy Boast, who had so far said nothing, cried excitedly, 'That's the way to treat 'em!' and knocked a jug of water into Mrs Lomax's lap. Mrs Lomax screamed; Bill Coke strode noisily through the saloon doors; the conversation at every table ceased; the band paused discordantly in the middle of a bar.

Ebbs was sitting with his head in his hands.

'Ladies and gentlemen…' He stood up dazedly. 'Please excuse… please…'

He hurried miserably away, at the doorway tripping headlong over his suspender.

7

Ebbs sat alone in his cabin feeling he had been thrown into a tank of icy water and was painfully beginning to thaw. His mess-jacket lay sprawled on the sofa, his tie and collar were scattered on the deck, his shoes were kicked into the corners, and his suspenders was still undone.

After a long time he reached for a pencil and sheet of ship's writing paper from his desk. He began drafting his resignation. He would post it at Suez, and at least forestall his certain dismissal at Fremantle. He was a failure. What Sir Angus had implied, his officers has suspected, and he himself had secretly feared, was true. After lumbering so long in floating pantechnicons round the rough ocean byways of the world, he was as useless for directing the *Charlemagne's* social life as the *Martin Luther's* engines for propelling her. For twenty-five years he had kept his sanity at sea by picturing himself one day presiding over dinner in the first-class saloon of a Pole Star liner. And what had happened? The greatest maritime fiasco since *The Wreck of the Hesperus*.

There was a soft tap at the jalousie, and Burtweed entered with a tray.

'Some tea and sandwiches, sir,' he volunteered. 'You didn't have much to eat in the saloon.'

'What's the time?' Ebbs asked gloomily.

'Just on eleven, sir.'

Ebbs watched him in silence as he set out the crockery.

'Dinner was not much of a success tonight, I fear, Burtweed.'

'I shouldn't let a little thing like that worry you, sir,' he replied with respectfully controlled cheerfulness. 'People act proper queer at sea sometimes.'

'It is hardly a "little thing",' Ebbs said miserably. 'It worries me considerably. My authority aboard has suffered a severe blow. What do you suppose the passengers will say? What do you imagine the office will think? I shall be ruined, Burtweed, as soon as news of this gets back to London.

'Why, bless us, sir, they'll have forgotten it tomorrow!'

Burtweed smiled on Ebbs like a mother with a bruised child. 'Very short, memories at sea, sir. They'll have so much to gossip about in a day or two they won't even give it a thought. Time and time again I've seen it, sir – they're all bosom pals north of Suez, and by the time we reach Sydney they've forgotten the names of the ones what got off at Melbourne. A ship is like Heaven, I always say,' Burtweed continued sunnily. 'The passengers come up the gangway – they might be anyone. They leave us in Australia – they might be going anywhere. In between, they all sort of get a fresh start, sir, to behave like they've always wanted to. That's why they plays up.'

'I hardly feel inclined to show my face in the saloon again,' Ebbs interrupted, as he had not been listening. 'I suppose nothing like this ever happened to Captain Buckle?'

'Oh, much worse, sir!' Burtweed said with enthusiasm. 'I remember two Italian singing gentlemen what we was taking out to Melbourne to perform, sir. They both became attracted to the same young lady, and when it got proper hot in the Red Sea they tried to do each other in with their butter-knives at lunch.'

'Open violence at least was avoided,' Ebbs murmured with faint gratitude.

'And don't forget, sir, tomorrow's the Captain's cocktail party.'

Ebbs groaned.

'I shouldn't give up, sir,' Burtweed said, carefully planting his last goad. 'After all, it's just part of the Captain's job, sir, isn't it? Like logging the crew if they're drunk, sir. You may not like it, but you have to take it as it comes. With respect, sir.'

Ebbs sighed. 'In a way you're right, Burtweed. I obviously cannot desert my post in the middle of the voyage. Whether it's in the wheelhouse or in the saloon.' He thought for a few moments, looking as if he was deciding to shoot a favourite dog. 'I suppose I can sleep on it,' he declared.

'That's the spirit, sir!'

'Anyway, I must go to the bridge and write my night orders.' He wearily began putting on his collar. 'Whatever the state of the ship's social life, her navigation must continue. Then I shall turn in. At least I have the consolation that my troubles of today are over.'

Ebbs had a captain's gift of falling asleep immediately but waking at the faintest interruption in the calm rhythm of a ship's night. After dreaming repeatedly that he was racing down the *Charlemagne's* boat deck stark naked with Lady McWhirrey, he suddenly sat up in bed. There was a noise outside, in his day-cabin. He listened again. A knock, short and timid, sounded at his outer door. He scrambled to the deck, reached for his mothy woollen dressing-gown and soap-spattered slippers, switched on his day-cabin light, and opened the door beyond. In the alleyway outside stood Annette Porter-Williams and Mr Dancer, hand in hand and looking sheepish.

'I say,' said Dancer. He laughed nervously. 'I wonder – that is, can you marry us?'

Ebbs looked at them blankly for some seconds. He pulled a handkerchief from his dressing-gown pocket and blew his nose.

'Do I understand that you wish me to perform the – ah, wedding ceremony?' he asked, as if it were some surgical operation.

'That's right,' Dancer said. 'Straight away.' The couple shot shy glances at each other and giggled.

'Come inside,' Ebbs said.

Still hand in hand, they stood in the centre of his cabin.

'But why couldn't you have got married before you came on board?' he asked, puzzled.

'Why, we didn't know each other then.'

'You mean – you are intending on the strength of a few days' acquaintance – '

'Not even a few days, Captain.' Dancer laughed again.

He was a thin, handsome young man with pale hair and neat teeth. 'We only really met this evening at dinner,' he explained. 'At your table, you know. But we got along jolly well, you see, and…and…do you believe in fate, Captain?'

Ebbs, who was smoothing down his hair, shook his head discouragingly.

'Well, out there on the boat-deck,' Dancer went on, 'with the stars and the moon, you know, and the sea rushing far below, and Annette's hair glittering in the lights… ' He was suddenly gripped by the memory of powerful emotion. 'I realised all at once…we both realised, that is…didn't we, darling?' he gasped, squeezing her hand vigorously.

'Angel one!' she murmured. They went into a robust embrace.

Ebbs had heard all about shipboard romances, but the speed of this one seemed to him more appropriate to the farmyard.

'I'm afraid you find me somewhat unprepared for this situation,' he said, wondering what to do next. 'I have for many years been a confirmed bachelor, and know very little about such things. However, I suppose it's my duty as the ship's Captain to comply with your request. As long as it is perfectly correct and proper, of course.'

They were taking no notice of him, so he reached for the heavy copy of *Company Regulations* standing next to the flag-emblazoned ship's Bible in his bookcase. He opened it hoping the authors had a wide view of the emergencies likely to beset a Captain at sea. Ebbs was a kind-hearted man who pleasurably gave large subscriptions for his shipmates' wedding presents, but at the moment he wanted to go back to bed and thought he had never before seen such a revolting pair of people.

'I'm afraid I can't be much use to you,' he announced flicking over the pages. 'It's nothing more than a popular superstition that Captains can marry couples at sea. Look, it says so here.' He pointed out he paragraph, feeling greatly relieved.

Their faces fell.

'Oh, no, Captain!'

'But how utterly beastly!'

'I say,' Dancer said, animated with a bright idea. 'Couldn't we wake up one of those parson blokes on board?' Or all six of them, if it would make any difference?'

'I'm afraid that wouldn't be the slightest use either, Mr Dancer. Marriages simply aren't allowed to be solemnised aboard merchant ships at sea. I've read the regulation most carefully, I assure you. Some sort of licence would be necessary for the ship. Like the fumigation certificate,' he explained.

They looked like children denied sweets.

'I might possibly be permitted to call the banns at sea,' Ebbs said, thumbing over more pages in the hope of offering them some consolation. 'Perhaps something could then be fixed up in Port Said or Aden – there seems to be plenty of British clergy in both places.'

'But I want to get married tonight!' cried Annette. Then she burst into tears.

'God help us!' Ebbs muttered. He suddenly thought fondly of the *Martin Luther*: there he had been hauled from his bunk almost nightly through some mechanical or navigational fault, but at least it was impossible for his cabin to be invaded by hysterical women at three in the morning.

'But my dear young lady,' Ebbs said patiently. 'It is only a matter of waiting a couple of days. What on earth do you want to get married tonight for?'

'How dare you, sir!' Dancer snapped, to Ebbs' astonishment. 'I'll have you know that Annette is a thoroughly respectable girl!'

'My dear sir, my dear sir!' Ebbs exclaimed, blushing deeply. 'I assure you I didn't mean to imply… I mean to think that you… ' He swallowed. 'I only meant to say that the courtship has been somewhat brief, and a day or so's reflection… '

'You do, do you?' Dancer removed his consoling arms from Annette and faced Ebbs squarely. 'You imply, I suppose, Captain, that Annette and I are making a mistake? You mean that tomorrow morning we shall discover we don't love each other? I see. You are telling me, in fact, that the sweetest and most wonderful woman in the world – '

'No, no, no!' Ebbs cried. 'I assure you I meant nothing of the – '

'I will have you know, Captain,' Dancer continued aggressively, 'that there is not, never has been, and never possibly can be, another woman in the world for me but Annette.' Annette had subsided into snuffles, but at this declaration she began to cry loudly again. 'To suggest that our love is not true, strong, and enduring is an insult to the dearest woman on earth. I realise you are the Captain of this ship, sir, and even as a passenger I must show you some respect. But by God! Anyone else I'd be inclined to give a punch on the nose – '

'Mr Dancer! Have you taken leave of your senses?' Ebbs shouted. 'What is all this nonsense? You come to my cabin in the middle of the night with a most unreasonable request, to say the least, and I am doing my best to help you – '

'I meant no offence,' Dancer said, soothed by the return of Annette to his damp shirt-front. 'After all ' he went on more tolerantly, 'I suppose if it hadn't been for you, and sitting at your table, and all that, we should never have met at all. Should we, my dearest one? All my future happiness would have been absolutely lost. It's a breathtaking thought.'

'Quite. Well, you must reconcile yourself to the fact that I cannot unite you in holy matrimony at the moment. You must therefore – ah, possess your souls in patience. Now I should, if you please, like to go back to bed.' Ebbs paused. He remembered for the first time his last interview in London. McWhirrey wanted romance, and he was getting it. 'I think I should make some formal announcement to the ship,' he continued more benignly. 'My cocktail party is tomorrow evening, and that seems a highly appropriate occasion. You are both asked, I trust? Good. Then I shall do everything in my power to arrange the wedding for the moment we reach Port Said. And now let me take the opportunity of offering you – perhaps somewhat belatedly – my heartiest congratulations and best wishes.'

The couple, beginning to smile again, stood hand in hand before him.

'No doubt,' Ebbs went on, trying to enter into the spirit of the thing, 'you will require a ring. Possibly they are obtained at the ship's hairdresser's – they sell all sorts of things.'

'I have one!' Annette said breathlessly. She pulled a ring from her right hand and dropped it on *Company Regulations*, which Ebbs was holding open in front of him.

'Now, Mr Dancer,' Ebbs said, becoming faintly coy. 'I believe you place it on the third finger of the left hand.'

'I say!' Dancer exclaimed. He looked happily at Ebbs and took the ring. 'It's almost a wedding, isn't it?' I mean – you, the ring, the book…all that's necessary now is for you to give us your blessing.'

Ebbs closed *Company Regulations* with a snap. 'Certainly not, Mr Dancer!' he said severely. 'I will not take responsibility for your actions. Good night!'

8

'Let us pray,' said Canon Swingle.

Ebbs reverently lowered his head, and began keenly inspecting the rows of passengers under his eyebrows.

It was the next morning, a Sunday, and the news had run through the ship like a fire alarm that Ebbs was in a black mood. He had woken into the unsettled climate between the past thunderclouds of yesterday's dinner and the coming turmoil of the cocktail party; his sleep had been broken into by a pair of amorous idiots; he had cut himself shaving, his breakfast was cold, he had made a foolish mistake calculating the ship's morning position, and he had found pile of cigarette-ends behind the flag-locker on the bridge. Ebbs was a mild man, but any one of these occurrences at sea is usually sufficient to turn the delicate balance of a Captain's liver.

As Ebbs' only acquaintance with the prayer-book in the past twenty-five years had been on the disposal of his dead shipmates, he had deputed command of the *Charlemagne's* spiritual navigation to Canon Swingle. The Canon now stood between himself and Shawe-Wilson at a flag-draped table in the first-class lounge, giving the service the professional polish of his practised monotone. He was a lean, vague man of the type often found desiccating in English cathedrals, and had been stimulated by his surroundings and large captive congregation to decorate his supplications with the rich hand of a Victorian architect.

'Like this so fragile bark which bears us all,' he insisted, 'we uncertainly navigate the currents of this life. We barely miss the perilous headland and rocky cape, we foolishly scrape shoal and sandbank, and we lie helpless in storm and tempest, fearful for our brittle hull and feeble decks. We are blind to the lighthouse and deaf to the foghorn, lost, unable to steer, searching for the miracle of the joyous harbour… '

This idiot doesn't say much for my navigation, Ebbs thought, folding his arms.

They rose to sing *For Those in Peril on the Sea* (Ebbs had vetoed *Nearer My God to Thee* as traditionally reserved for the ship disappearing beneath them) while Mutt and Jeff passed round cocktail salvers for the collection with their special Sunday expressions of piety. Church is always well attended by ship's passengers, less from a resort to religion because of the insecure environment than the lack of alternative amusements on Sunday mornings and the impossibility of staying in bed. Ebbs stared over his *Ancient and Modern*, trying to spy out the members of his table. Annette and Dancer had their fingers entwined round a prayer-book, the Cokes now sang like two harmonious angels, and Mrs Porteous interrupted her careful expression of sanctity by shooting sharp glances at Shawe-Wilson and himself. Mrs Judd had been asked to play the piano for the hymns, and Brigadier Broster was standing in the front row, looking disagreeable. The Canon gave a address which lasted for twenty-five minutes, then everyone sang the National Anthem and hurried below to reinforce the glow of righteousness with their morning gin. The ensign was lowered from the *Charlemagne's* stern, the collection was counted and turned over to the Purser roughly correct, and as far as the ship was concerned Sunday had expired.

Replacing their caps, Ebbs and Shawe-Wilson left the lounge for the Square, a space by the first-class sally ports containing the Purser's office and hairdresser's shop, which at sea became the market-place of ship's life, where notices could be posted, messages collected, girls eyed, and gossip exchanged.

'After my somewhat disturbed night I shall not be holding the customary Captain's Sunday inspection,' Ebbs announced, yawning. 'Instead I shall tour the ship informally by myself during the afternoon.'

'That won't be very popular with the crew, sir,' Shawe-Wilson said at once. 'They don't much like to have the Captain snooping on them.'

'If you will wait to hear the rest of my remarks,' Ebbs said patiently, 'perhaps you will spare me the benefit of your advice on how to command my ship. I wish you to inform all departments of my intentions, for the specific purpose of preventing anyone feeling "snooped on", as you say.'

'Captain Buckle usually left inspection and so forth to me, sir.'

'Captain Buckle, I do not wish to remind you, is no longer with us.'

'Oh, quite, sir. I was only making a suggestion. I thought at the moment you would prefer to concentrate on learning to handle the passengers.'

'Mr Shawe-Wilson –!' Ebbs checked himself and blew his nose. He went on: 'I am perfectly confident of my ability to handle both the ship and the people in her – get that in your head, please, and keep it there.'

'Yes, sir.'

'If it comes to that, what about boat-drill? Under Company Regulations that is your responsibility. Why haven't we had boat-drill? We've been at sea almost a week.'

'The weather's been too rough, sir.'

'That answer, Mr Shawe-Wilson, would sound ridiculous in a court of inquiry. We shall exercise crew and passengers to boat stations at four o'clock.'

'But it's Sunday, sir.'

'I was not aware, Mr Shawe-Wilson, that your religious principles extended so far.'

'We can't have boat-drill on a Sunday, sir. It's the passengers' afternoon whist drive.'

'I don't care if it's the passengers' afternoon washing day. Boat-drill at four.'

'I can tell you that the passengers will be extremely disappointed, sir,' the Chief Officer said.

'Damn it, Mr Shawe-Wilson! The safety of the ship comes first, doesn't it? I am the Captain, aren't I?'

'Yes, sir…'

'Boat-drill then, Mr Shawe-Wilson. At four. And what the devil are you doing here?'

The last remark arrested Jay, the Fourth Officer, like a lasso. He was hurrying down the stairs from the deck in his Sunday uniform, without noticing Ebbs.

'You are aware that Company Regulations forbid junior officers the passengers' decks?' Ebbs thundered.

Jay opened his mouth. He stood with his shoulders hunched, gripping the edge of his jacket, rubbing his left ankle with his right heel. He was at the age and rank to be genuinely scared of all Captains.

'Was going to mark the noon position on the passengers' chart, sir,' Jay mumbled. In fact, he had an appointment in the starboard ironing-room after Church with a red-headed girl, achieved after a painfully ingenious passage of notes.

'The time now, Mr Jay, is eleven-fifteen.'

Jay tried to express sound.

'Kindly return to your quarters immediately. Purser,' Ebbs went on, as Jay scuttled above like a frightened squirrel. 'I should like to see your bar account books, if you please.'

'With the greatest of pleasure, sir.' Prittlewell knew that whenever a Captain woke in a bad mood he wanted to see the bar account books. 'I'll bring them up to your cabin at once.'

'That is the general running balance,' Prittlewell said a few minutes later, covering Ebbs' desk with open ledgers. 'You see here, these figures are only corrected against the profit and loss under the imprest system, but the above-the-line items will be set down among the entries made in the following account, because we can strike only a mean balance and – '

'It looks rather complicated,' Ebbs said moodily. 'In the *Luther* we did it all in an exercise book and I kept it in my drawer.'

'Rather a bigger problem here, sir,' Prittlewell said, polishing his monocle.

'Well, I must confess these figures don't mean much to me,' Ebbs admitted. He always felt uncomfortable in the presence of the Purser, who was beginning to remind him of his sister. 'I'd better take your word that everything's correct.'

Prittlewell smiled. 'I assure you, sir, I have hardly robbed a till for years – '

'I certainly had no intention of casting aspersions on your honesty.'

'I'm sure you didn't, sir. Perhaps if you'll sign the page, as required by Company Regulations…'

Ebbs took out his pen.

'And if you'd like to sign these blank pages too, sir, I shan't have to bother you again till the end of the voyage. 'Thank you, sir,' he said, as Ebbs blotted the last signature. 'Most obliging of you. We shall meet again tonight then, sir? I am sure your cocktail party will be a great success.'

'Let us hope it will be an improvement on last night's dinner,' Ebbs said. 'I shall do my best to co-operate.'

'I'm sure you will, sir. You are quite the most co-operative Captain I've sailed with for some time. Good morning, sir.'

During most of the day Ebbs stayed in his cabin. He had decided not to resign until he had played a return match with his passengers at the cocktail party, but he was still too ashamed to face any of them alone. Meanwhile they were settling themselves into the customary pattern of shipboard society. The traditional friendships were forged, at all temperatures from the white heat of passion to the tepid coincidence of occupying different ends of the same English county, and companions rapidly coalesced into cliques: the gossips settled in their steamer-chairs and began their daily speculation in the busy market of ship's scandal, the athletes strode their calculated miles, and the bridge players held their sovereign corner of the lounge and played steadily on each other's nerves.

Of the *Charlemagne's* complement the most serious set were her band of drinkers – five or six well-seasoned men who travelled often and looked upon ships mainly as liberal dispensaries for duty-free liquors. They had been marshalled from their lonely corners of the smoke-room under the captaincy of Mr Willy Boast, a companionable man whom the long cricketing summers had left permanently parched. At ten in the morning they found their leathery nest beside the smoke-room bar, waiting for the rattle of Scottie's shutter to rise on the dawn of their day. They first exchanged a few words of gently jocular conversation about the state of health and liver, but these were only estimable asides like Prayers in the

House of Commons. Mutt and Jeff shortly appeared unsummoned with the usual round of eye-openers, which were followed by sun-papers, bracers, stiffeners, and snorts, until the drinkers were forced to scatter uncertainly to their cabins when the bar shut under ship's regulations at three. Mr Boast then wrapped a wet towel round his head and infuriated his neighbours by rattling a few pages of his next book *Completely Stumped* from his portable typewriter, in the way that he composed his famous cricketing pieces for his newspaper on long licensed afternoons in country pavilions. He continued writing steadily till five, when the bar reopened and his companions met again to tipple purposefully into the evening, ending with their final sundowners, night-caps, tiger-frighteners, shark-scarers, and porpoise-chasers as Scottie's shutter guillotined their conviviality at midnight.

At four o'clock that afternoon this lazy ship's routine was cut by the whistle blowing Abandon Ship, and the passengers came sheepishly up the ladders in their life-jackets to boat stations. The only exceptions were Willy Boast, who had locked himself in his cabin, and old Mrs Lomax, who misheard her stewardess' assurance and came screaming on deck, bald, toothless, and in her corsets.

The passengers gathered on the promenade deck in the charge of Shawe-Wilson, who strode among them with his cap sharply over one eye and his thumbs jutting from his jacket pockets: boat-drill was his favourite item of sea-going duty.

'Now just listen to me a minute,' he began sternly to the assembly. Respectful silence fell. 'If anything should happen to the ship,' he continued with impressive offhandedness, 'I don't want any panic. You know the form – women and children first. There's no danger if everyone keeps his head. You can take that from me. I saw that clear enough when I was torpedoed. Every time.' He eyed the thoroughly subjected audience austerely. 'Everyone will wait for orders. I don't want any rushing the boats in any circumstances. Remember you're British. Or Australian,' he added quickly. 'Now you –' He picked the prettiest girl in sight. 'Do you know how to put on a life-jacket in five seconds?'

She blushed, and shook her head, as if he had publicly accused her of immorality.

'In that case, I'd better demonstrate. Everyone gather round me, please – you may smoke if you wish – and I'll show you the way we put on our life-jackets in the Service. Now, young lady, if you will stand here, immediately in front of me, and give me both your hands… '

On the boat-deck above, Brickwood came up the bridge ladder, saluted, and said to Ebbs, 'Boats secure, sir.'

'Very good, Mr Brickwood. All hands seem to know their job. I am perfectly satisfied with the conduct of the exercise.'

'Thank you, sir. Shall I blow Dismiss?'

'We'd better wait for Mr Shawe-Wilson to finish with the passengers, hadn't we?'

'Aye aye, sir.'

Ebbs paced the bridge, thinking about the cocktail party. He had never looked forward to a function with such disrelish since his initiation to the sea, when his fellow-cadets had arranged a cabin celebration at which he was to provide the main entertainment by swallowing a mug of sea-water laced with Epsom salts and treacle while standing on one leg in the nude and singing *Rule Britannia*. He decided he wouldn't make the mistake of last night's dinner by plotting his course in advance: he would treat the affair like a typhoon, and manoeuvre as the moment's peril dictated. And if the guests looked like getting out of hand he could always retire to his bathroom and lock himself in until they had gone.

'Hasn't Mr Shawe-Wilson finished yet?' he asked impatiently, ten minutes later.

'He's very thorough, sir.' Said Brickwood.

Ebbs spent another five minutes fussing round the horizon with his glasses, then exclaimed: 'Damnation! What can the fellow be doing? We can't keep the whole ship's company waiting like this. Mr Brickwood!'

'Sir?'

'Kindly take charge up here,'

'Aye, aye, sir.'

Ebbs strode to the ladder leading to the promenade deck, glared down, and found Shawe-Wilson demonstrating a reef-knot across the umbilicus of a warmly co-operative blonde.

'Mr Shawe-Wilson,' he said later, when the Chief Officer had been brought to the bridge by the tactful summons of a Quartermaster. 'Is it necessary for you to instruct the passengers in boat-drill so – ah, intimately?'

'It seems important to me to show them how to put on a life-jacket, sir,' he said blandly.

'Precisely. But you could perhaps have demonstrated as effectively on a Quartermaster?'

'I think I might say, sir, that Sir Angus McWhirrey personally congratulated me on the way I handled the passengers at boat-drill.'

'Mr Shawe-Wilson,' said Ebbs deliberately. 'You have the unfortunate knack of bringing me every few hours to the edge of my temper. Isn't there anything you can do about it? I know you look on me as a dithering old fool, but you ought to know by now it's the Chief Officer's job to put up with dithering old fools. Is there any reason why we shouldn't work perfectly harmoniously together?'

Shawe-Wilson stuck out his lower lip.

'Of course there isn't,' Ebbs went on. 'I have difficulties enough in the ship already, as I'm sure you know only too well. Let us bury the hatchet, please. This evening at my cocktail party seems an eminently suitable occasion. There is no reason why you and I should not get along splendidly.' He blew his nose. 'A fresh start, if you please, Mr Shawe-Wilson. As for now, I will say no more. Kindly signal Dismiss.'

9

The Captain's cocktail party officially set spinning the *Charlemagne's* social whirl, and the treasured invitations slipped under selected cabin doors had the standing on board of a summons to Buckingham Palace. The party was traditionally held in the Captain's cabin, which caused noticeable conflict between the Pole Star Line's marine architecture and its social conscience: as every voyage there was an increasing number of people the Line felt obliged to invite, and as Captain's suite any larger would have given the ship the look of a houseboat, after half an hour the host was generally reminded of the foc's'le of a Liverpool coal-burner on a still night in the tropics, when the firemen had just emerged from stokehold watch.

At five that evening Burtweed made it plain to Ebbs that he was dispossessed of his quarters, by arriving with four assistant stewards bearing dishes of canapés, *paté de foie gras*, and caviar sandwiches. Ebbs obediently retreated to his night-cabin to change. His feelings about the party by then were mixed: be devoutly wished the next few hours were over, but after a lifetime of sharply questioned repair bills and niggardly store lists even the flintiest Captain would have found the opportunity of playing lavish host with his Company's money irresistibly attractive.

As he emerged from his shower he found a letter awaiting him.

'From the religious gentleman, sir,' Burtweed explained.

Dear Captain [Ebbs read], I must ask you to excuse me from your cocktail party tonight. I cannot tolerate being in the same room as Brigadier Broster. I do not much like being in the same ship with him, but unmercifully there is no alternative. I admit I am only a Canon of the Church of England, but I cannot agree that the Brigadier would have taken this morning's service any better. He believes this to be the case. He also spent the afternoon instructing me in various points of doctrine. Apparently he does this as a matter of course in his own village, where the incumbent has my sincere sympathy.

Yours sincerely,

A R T Swingle

PS. I much dislike craving favours, but would it be possible to move me to another table for my meals? I have invested almost my last penny in this trip, as my doctor said I needed a complete change.

Ebbs sighed, and stuck the letter behind his mirror. It was consoling to know other people had their troubles as well.

'Welcome, gentlemen, welcome,' he said a little later, appearing in his mess-kit in the day-cabin. 'Very pleased to see you, gentlemen, and very grateful for your encouragement.'

His senior officers, who pillared the responsibility of the party with him, were already standing among the glass and silver savouring their first free drinks. There was Prittlewell and Shawe-Wilson; Earnshawe, the Chief Engineer, a red-faced Yorkshireman with hands like elephants' ears; and the ship's doctor, a charming elderly practitioner who had retired to the unexacting practice of the sea after a lifetime of equally tranquil therapy for the Bengal railways.

'I trust this evening will denote the beginning of a more fruitful comradeship between us,' Ebbs said with more assurance than he felt. 'All ships are the same, gentlemen, but they take time to settle down. They have their stresses and strains – if I may borrow an expression from your department, Mr Earnshawe. But we shall certainly need your support – to give me a hand with the ladies, eh, Mr Shawe-Wilson?' Shawe-Wilson winced. 'You've made quite a spread, Purser, quite a spread,' Ebbs continued, surveying the sandwiches benignly. 'What are these little fellows here? By the way, Purser, you'd better shift the Canon again. Put him with those young lady gymnasts – very appetising sandwich, this, very appetising indeed!'

'So they ought to be, sir. They cost the Company about five shillings each.'

'Really? Five shillings? Well, Purser, I am surprised! Who'd have thought you could pay five shillings for a sandwich? What on earth can – '

'Commander and Mrs Barker!' announced Burtweed from the door.

'Good gracious, guests already!' Ebbs exclaimed, springing across the cabin with outstretched hand.

Shawe-Wilson looked at the others. 'Caviar for the – er, Captain,' he murmured.

Commander Barker greeted Ebbs heartily, recognised the cut of his jib, and asked if they had met in the Bombay Yacht Club, the Royal Thames Yacht Club, or the Royal Yacht Squadron. Ebbs murmured that he didn't belong to any clubs and had never been in a yacht, and passed quickly to the next arrival. The guests were already queuing in the alleyway outside, and were admitted under the regulating eye of Burtweed while Ebbs stood at the door distributing the small currency of politeness with progressive generosity. As he had hardly looked further than the passengers who ringed him in the dining saloon, he greeted most of them as strangers; but shortly he began to find old friends.

'Dear Captain!' Mrs Porteous, in a tight low-cut dress, took his hand warmly. 'How terribly sweet of you to ask me to your perfectly lovely party.'

'I assure you, madam, the pleasure – '

'You have such deep, deep, grey eyes,' she murmured, squeezing his fingers and looking up at him. 'I suppose you're always standing on the bridge searching for things? How tired you must get!'

Across the cabin, Shawe-Wilson raised his eyebrows. Her look, foreign to Ebbs, was expertly translated by himself.

'Yes, indeed, of course,' Ebbs mumbled, looking round for relief. 'Ah, Purser! The Purser here will see to your refreshment,' he continued, handling her on. 'There are jolly nice sandwiches, and so forth. My dear Mr Boast,' he continued immediately, through the door. 'How very good of you to tear yourself away from your literary labours.'

'Jolly old pals,' said Mr Boast amiably.

The cabin filled, the chattering increased, the officers circulated the silver dishes with practised grace, and the stewards began to sweat into the Martinis. Before long it looked like any other cocktail party: people began shouting at each other, ignoring their partner's conversation, and laughing loudly at their own jokes, while the women began being catty and the men shot hot glances of appraisal at the girls across the room.

Shawe-Wilson shortly withdrew from the noisy core of guests and leaned thoughtfully with his pink gin on the bulkhead. The night of the Captain's cocktail party was a critical one for him, for it signalled the start of his amorous activities on board. He was a tidy gallant, who had reserved the first five or six days at sea to assess the applicants for his attentions ever since his maiden voyage in the *Charlemagne*, when he had thoughtlessly grabbed the first girl presenting herself as the ship cleared Dover and had journeyed restlessly to Sydney in her embraces. Now he preferred a more sportive attachment until the ship reached the Red Sea, and he could choose a second companion to last until the Australian coast. This time-table was subject to instant cancellation directly a more rewarding target presented itself, for Shawe-Wilson was the sort of man who could never mentally undress a girl without simultaneously valuing her clothes. He had no intention of pacing a bridge for the rest of his life, and had decided to obtain his discharge from the sea by the first heiress who happened to travel in the *Charlemagne*. Twice he had smelt success: but the first girl's father suddenly went bankrupt and shot himself, and the second, the only daughter of a brewing millionaire, called him Boykins and was as graceless as a combine harvester.

'About the lot, sir,' Burtweed muttered in Ebbs' ear.

Ebbs nodded. No disaster of protocol had yet occurred, and he was beginning to think of himself guardedly as a social success. 'All goes well?' he said hopefully.

'Very decent, sir.'

'I shall circulate among the guests, then. That's the thing to do, I take it?'

He squeezed into the cabin with the intention of passing himself round like an animated canapé. He was jostled from group to group, his drink unsipped in his hand, making awkward pleasantries like a clergyman being genial in a pub. But his guests received him respectfully enough, and politely kept the conversation to technical questions about the sea. Who did the steering while he was having his lunch? Did he sleep in a hammock?

How many times had he been shipwrecked? Do rats really desert a sinking ship? Was it true about sailors having a girl in every port? Was he born in a caul? The men all called him sir and apologised lavishly when they spilt their drinks down his uniform, and everyone offered him more politeness than the legal measure he managed to extract from his officers under the Merchant Shipping Acts. Ebbs found it all modestly encouraging.

"My, Captain!' Gwenny said, as the mercurial Cokes penned him in a corner. 'This is the nicest party we've had since we left Sydney! Isn't it, Bill?'

'I trust the breaches of last night,' Ebbs asked sheepishly, 'are healed?'

They looked at him.

'Just a lovers' tiff,' Bill Coke explained, through a mouthful of sandwich. 'Gwenny and me are sort of – well, high spirited. Why, she's the sweetest girl that ever crossed Sydney Bridge, and that's saying something.'

'My, isn't that nice? Do you know what, Captain?' Gwenny giggled. 'This is a second honeymoon for us.'

'Excellent!' said Ebbs, beginning to feel the *Charlemagne's* memories truly did fade away as swiftly as her wake. 'Just what the Company intended.'

'And we reckon you're a pretty good sport, too, Captain.'

Ebbs bowed modestly in recognition of the supreme Australian compliment.

'Though the first time we saw you,' her husband went on, neatly whipping a drink off a passing tray, 'we thought you was a proper Pommy bastard. Didn't we, Gwenny?'

'Too right we did! I said to Bill, "What do you reckon to the Captain?" And he said, "Gwenny, he looks like a sick cow in a stiff shirt." Didn't you, Bill?'

'That's just what I said, Gwenny love.'

'Quite,' Ebbs said.

Then suddenly the fragile raft of confidence on which he floated began to sink beneath his feet. 'In England,' he heard behind him, 'we travel for pleasure. We do not do journeys simply to get to places in the shortest possible time. We have our motor cars – very large and comfortable motor cars – and our chauffeurs. We English are great travellers. In winter, we visit the south of France, or Madeira, or Malta, or possibly the winter sports. In summer, we tour Scotland, or our West Country, or Wales. I – ah, Captain!' Broster continued as the perversity of the party brought Ebbs within six inches of his nose. 'I'd like a word with you.'

'Yes, Brigadier?'

'I don't want to claim any special privileges on board. You know that. I'm just an ordinary passenger like the rest. The fact that I own half the Line doesn't make the slightest difference. You understand?'

'Very considerate of you, sir.'

'But it utterly astonishes me that I haven't been asked to serve on the ship's sports committee. I've had particularly wide experience of this sort of thing and I know the ropes. Every other Captain I've sailed with has been after me like a shot. Of course, it's entirely a matter for you, and I should be the last to interfere with your running the ship. But to be overlooked completely I can only describe as a – '

'I shall see to it that your services are made use of at the earliest possible moment,' Ebbs said. 'It is kind of you to suggest it,' he added stiffly.

'Another thing. The tap in my cabin goes drip-drip-drip all the blasted night. Haven't had a wink of sleep since leaving Tilbury. And judging from the smell coming out of my ventilator, something must have crawled up there and died. It's not that I'm complaining – '

'I'll have both repaired during dinner.'

'I might as well tell you, 'Broster said, fixing Ebbs with a meaningful stare, 'that McWhirrey asked me *to keep an eye on you.*'

'Really?' Ebbs gave a brave and flabby smile. 'I sincerely trust...I sincerely hope... I assure you there will be no – ah, no cause, no cause whatever... '

He tried to back away through a pair of guests and found himself jammed between Mrs Porteous and the bulkhead.

'I knew you'd struggle over to me!' she said with delight. 'How perfectly sweet of you, Captain!' As Ebbs caught Broster's eye across her naked shoulder, she lowered her voice. 'Darling,' she whispered. 'Do come and pay me a little visit tonight, won't you? My cabin's A25 – I'll be waiting for you at midnight.'

Ebbs dropped his glass.

She gripped his arm. 'Promise?' she breathed.

'Impossible!' he hissed. 'Preposterous! Good God, woman!'

'But *promise*, darling!'

'Miss Annette Porter-Williams!' boomed Burtweed from the door.

Ebbs gasped.

'Please come, darling!'

'Let me go, let me go!' He tugged his arm away and pushed through the cabin. He arrived breathless at the doorway. 'Miss Porter-Williams – er, Miss, er, my dear,' he greeted her. 'I – ah, how do you do?'

'Lovely party!' she said, smiling round. 'Are we beastly late?'

'Burtweed!' Ebbs called hastily. He forcefully collected himself. 'Silence, if you please.'

'Ladies and gentlemen!' Burtweed shouted, as if hailing the crow's-nest. 'Pray silence for the Captain.'

As the conversation died Ebbs shakily drew from his pocket a ship's postcard, on which he had written in red ink a short dignified speech.

'Ladies and gentlemen,' he began, slipping the card out of sight. 'A Captain has many varied duties in a voyage, some pleasant, some not so pleasant. But this is one of the more pleasant ones. It is very pleasant for me to have the – ah, pleasure, that is…the engagement, which I now announce, with great pleasure, between Miss Annette Porter-Williams and – ' He looked up. Annette was stroking the cheek of a carroty-haired youth he had never seen before. 'What's this?' he hissed. 'Where's Dancer?'

'He was beastly,' she explained.

'You mean…you mean… ' Ebbs pointed anxiously. 'You're engaged to…?'

'The name's Muggs, of Brisbane. I popped the question this afternoon – right out there on the deck-tennis court. My oath, you could have knocked me down with a sandbag when little Annette accepted! She's a great kid,' he explained heartily to the audience. 'A great little kid. And will the old folks be surprised to see what I've brought home!'

'Lovely, lovely one!' Annette exclaimed, ruffling his hair.

Ebbs held a hand over his eyes. And now, he thought, more trouble at dinner.

10

When Ebbs returned to his cabin shortly before midnight he was a modestly contented man. The cocktail party had on the whole been a success. Dinner had followed naturally as a jovial meal, at which he was relieved to find himself almost completely ignored. Afterwards he had graced the adult snakes-and-ladders of the smoke-room race meeting, and he had proudly come away ten shillings ahead of the book.

'I really think I'm getting the hang of these passengers,' he announced cheerfully to Burtweed, who was gathering handbags, cigarette-lighters, and divorced earrings from the furniture with experienced thoroughness. 'Despite my somewhat disastrous start, from now on let's hope it's all going to be plain sailing.'

'I'm real glad, sir!' Burtweed said warmly. 'There's no one I'd wish success on more than you, sir. As I said to my mates down below, "The new Captain's a real gentleman," I said, sir. "You can tell that – not a foul word he's uttered and never been drunk once since we left Tilbury." '

'Thank you, Burtweed.' Ebbs yawned. 'Now I must go up to the bridge for my night orders. Kindly open the other scuttles – the place still smells like a lady's boudoir.'

'Very good, sir. Good night, sir.'

'Good night to you, Burtweed.'

As Ebbs climbed the ladder to the darkened chart-room abaft the bridge a deep ripple of peace ran through him. The *Charlemagne's* navigational equipment was neat and modern, with an automatic pilot, a shrunken wheel, and melodious electric telegraphs; but all ship's bridges retain the bewitching association of brass and teak, blackness and shaded light, tranquillity and unremitting watch, that can entice men away from the land for a lifetime. Here Ebbs felt secure, familiar, and paramount: the clamorous passengers were reduced to the inconsequential squawking of harbour gulls.

He went to the chart spread in a splash of hooded light and ran his finger thoughtfully along the faint pencil line that marked the *Charlemagne's* progress. Then he opened the small green-covered book labelled *Master's Night Orders* that every night represented him as he slept. He formally recorded the ship's position and course, filled a page with minor instruction and exhortation, and ended with the benediction 'All Company Regulations to be strictly observed. Signed: W Ebbs, Master.'

He closed the book and stepped into the black, gently-creaking wheelhouse. He stopped. He sniffed. He sniffed again. On the starboard wing of the bridge he could make out the double-headed shape of Bowels and Jay, the two officers keeping watch. As he looked, a glow briefly illuminated their faces and a guilty cone of sparks suddenly shot towards the sea.

Ebbs strode through the wheelhouse door. If anything irritated him more than blunt chartroom pencils, it was smoking on watch.

'Mr Jay,' he said sternly through the darkness. 'I will relieve you of the danger of setting fire to your trousers.'

Jay nervously drew his hand from his pocket and threw a lighted cigarette over the side.

'Are you aware,' Ebbs went on, 'that smoking on the bridge is expressly forbidden in Company Regulations? It is also utterly out of keeping with the etiquette of a British ship at sea. I trust I shall never play the martinet, gentlemen, but there are certain properties I insist on having observed. From smoking on the bridge it is but a short step to – ah, beer bottles in the chartroom and pontoon in the wheelhouse. I will not have it, gentlemen. I will not! Kindly understand that.'

'Captain Buckle – ' began Bowles, the Third Officer.

'Mr Bowles, must I tell you again that I am not in the slightest concerned with the conduct of the ship under Captain Buckle? In future, there is to be no smoking on the bridge. By anyone and at any time. Do you understand that?'

'Yes, sir,' Bowles said. He reflected sadly that all good skippers were the same, but the cranks were cranky in their own peculiar ways.

'And you, too, Mr Jay, appreciate it I hope?'

Jay had not yet grown into his shipmate's sophisticated attitude to angry Captains, and found their proximity always withdrew the power of speech. He tried to agree heartily, and made a short squeaking noise.

'What did you say?' asked Ebbs.

Jay squeaked again.

'Kindly do not chirp at me, Mr Jay,' Ebbs said crossly. 'This is no laughing matter. You will also remember your position, if you please. We will now say no more about it. I try to treat my officers like gentlemen, but if Company Regulations are persistently to be broken I shall be obliged to – ah, take steps. Carry on please, Mr Bowles.'

'Aye aye, sir.'

Eight bells rang out. Ebbs returned to the chartroom, reopened the Night Order Book, and added to his last sentence, 'particularly those concerning smoking on the bridge.' Brickwood then appeared at the head of the ladder to take the middle watch. He was dressed in a pair of green corduroys, a khaki drill tunic, a Paisley scarf, and suede boots. He nodded a politely cheerful 'Good evening, sir,' and marched through to the wheelhouse filling his pipe.

Ebbs blew his nose.

'Mr Brickwood!'

'Sir?'

'One moment if you please, Mr Brickwood.'

The Second Officer returned to the chartroom.

'You are four minutes late coming on watch,' Ebbs said, with the deliberation of a tolling bell.

Brickwood gave a guilty glance at the chartroom clock. 'So I am, sir!' But I don't think the Third Officer – '

'It is not a matter of the Third Officer or anyone else, Mr Brickwood,' Ebbs interrupted. 'If Company Regulations say you are to come on the bridge at midnight, at midnight precisely you appear. Furthermore, you appear to be dressed for attending the ship's fancy-dress dance instead of the serious business of taking a watch at sea. What, may I ask, is the reason for your outrageous and extremely unseamanlike appearance?'

Brickwood glanced down at his clothes in surprise. 'Oh, this rig, sir?' Captain Buckle said the middle watch keeper could dress for comfort – '

Ebbs suddenly thumped the chart-table in exasperation, bouncing the pair of pencils on to the deck.

'I don't care if you appeared on the bridge under the command of Captain Buckle stark naked!' he roared. 'I will not have my officers slopping about as if this were a Grimsby fishing boat. Go below and put on your uniform, Mr Brickwood. If you please, at once!'

'Yes, sir.' Brickwood looked startled, as if an old sheep had turned round and bitten him. 'Certainly, sir.'

Ebbs turned back to the Night Order Book, and added 'Also those concerning dress.' He then underlined the sentence twice, watched Bowles and Jay initial the page in silence, and disappeared down the ladder to the deck.

Ebbs was shaken. The contentment of his evening had been shattered by his own officers, who were now without doubt cursing him bountifully just out of earshot. He was a sensitive man, those awkward years as a junior officer had left him with an unusual dislike of upbraiding his inferiors; but he sensed equally sharply his duty to the Company of maintaining discipline. To dissipate his anger he decided to take a turn round the boat-deck before going to his cabin, and as an extra sedative he drew from his inside pocket the cigar Bill Coke had given him in a burst of alcoholic generosity at dinner.

For a while Ebbs leaned with his back on the rail, watching the haze from the funnel which intermittently dimmed the stars and listening to the gentle protest of the water against the sides of the intruding ship. It was a mild night, the boat-deck was deserted, and lit only by a few lights carefully shaded away from the bridge. Ebbs reflected that the *Charlemagne's* passengers made early to bed. He began to stroll casually aft, puffing his cigar and whimsically following the smoke as it hesitated and was snatched away by the breeze. Soon his peace of mind returned, and he began to hum a few bars of some private song.

A giggle, as furtive as a scampering rat, came from a dark nook in the upperworks. Ebbs paused. Straining his eyes into the recess, he caught the flash of a stocking. Immediately he strode down the deck, keeping his gaze well out to sea.

He stopped at the after end of the boat-deck, where he leaned on the rail and puffed primly at his cigar. A slap – sharp, sudden, and unmistakable – rang from the space between a pair of lifeboats. Ebbs frowned deeply. He continued his walk, but more slowly. A timid glance into the shadowy corner by the after fan-house caught a close unheeding couple; and he found similar pairs between the starboard lifeboats, in the niches round the engine-room hatchways, at the base of the funnel, and tucked under the ladders leading to his own quarters. He suddenly realised that the boat-deck was alive, like a peaceful summer hayfield with rabbits.

By the time he had returned to the forward end of the decks, Ebbs' discretion had flagged. He made for the bridge ladder with quick and noisy strides, intending to finish his smoke in his cabin. But with one hand on the rail he stopped. From the shadow of the companionway he heard a swift sigh, and he caught the sparkle of a white shirt-front and three bands of official gold braid.

'Umm,' Ebbs said.

He hurried up to the bridge, throwing his cigar scrupulously over the side. Brickwood, dressed in his best uniform with a white cap-cover and stiff collar, saluted smartly as he appeared and began saying cheerfully, 'All Company's Regulations being strictly observed, sir – '

'Yes, yes,' Ebbs said. 'Where's the stand-by Quartermaster?'

'On the monkey island, sir.'

'Tell him to present my compliments to the Chief Officer and request him to come to the bridge immediately. He will find him in the starboard boat-deck companionway.'

Shawe-Wilson appeared on the bridge looking furious. He had selected with great care at the party a lanky extroverted girl, the second trombone of the travelling gymnast's band. He was a careful spender, but he had invested in her almost a pound's worth of mixed liquors since dinner; he had succeeded in enticing her to the boat-deck for a stroll; and he had just brought further persuasion to the point of suggesting slipping into his cabin, when this Ebbs offered the highest insult of dragging him away from the arms of the woman he loved, or was confidently preparing to.

'You wanted me for something, sir?' he said stiffly. He had decided to pass off the affair with dignity.

'Mr Brickwood,' Ebbs commanded. 'Kindly go on to the wing of the bridge.'

'Aye aye, sir.'

Ebbs closed the chartroom door. 'Mr Shawe-Wilson,' he began. 'What, may I ask, are you up to?'

'I was taking the night air, sir.'

'Really? You come up here smeared with lipstick and stinking of gin and cheap scent – '

'Sir!'

' – looking as if you've just rolled out of a whore's bedroom – '

'I must ask you, sir, to moderate – '

'Moderate be damned!' Ebbs struck the chartroom table again, alarming Brickwood, who was just beyond the door. 'I take a walk round the deck before I turn in, and what do I see? Why the place is like Grant Road, Bombay! I've never heard of such things.'

'The morals of the passengers are no concern of ours, sir.'

'But the morals of the Chief Officer are very much a concern of mine. You realise, Mr Shawe-Wilson, that you have been breaking the most serious of the Company's Regulations? Do you? Do you, sir?'

Shawe-Wilson shrugged his shoulders. 'The Chief Officer has certain social obligations… '

'Social obligations! Good God!'

'Under Captain Buckle – '

'I don't – ' Ebbs checked himself. He paused, his fist already over the chart table. 'I am disappointed, Mr Shawe-Wilson,' he went on quietly. 'I was hoping that you and I might make a fresh start this evening. I shall have to think again, that's all. It sadden me considerably. Now it is very late, and I have had an extremely trying day. I have no wish to turn over such delicate subjects at this moment. Tempers and judgements become unreliable – things are said which might be very regrettable. I should therefore be obliged if you would retire. Alone, please.'

'As you wish, sir,' Shawe-Wilson said, as irritatingly as possible.

'And I shall require you to come to my cabin at nine in the morning.'

'Nine? All right, sir.'

'Good night, Mr Shawe-Wilson,' Ebbs said formally.

The Chief Officer made no reply.

Ebbs stood for some time alone in the chartroom. He had no intention of accepting defiance from anyone. But as it was impossible to get shot of an officer until the ship returned to London, he wished whole-heartedly that Shawe-Wilson would meet with some reasonably disabling accident. With a sigh he followed the Chief Officer slowly down the ladder to his own cabin, his steps heavy with the cares of conscientious authority. He switched on the light and shut the door. He sniffed disagreeably: the perfume of the party still hung in the air. He slipped off his heavy mess-jacket with relief – it was always good to suspend the obligations of command by sleep. On an afterthought, he crossed to the cocktail cabinet and poured himself a small whisky and soda, which he took through to his night-cabin. He turned on the light, to find Mrs Porteous lying on his bed.

'Lord Almighty!' Ebbs said.

She giggled. 'I thought you were never coming, Captain dear.'

Ebbs put the glass down firmly on his dressing-table.

'My dear good woman,' he said. 'I really must request you to leave this cabin immediately.'

'Now, now, darling!' She pouted in playful reproach. 'That isn't the way to welcome a girl, is it?'

'Mrs Porteous – '

'Elspeth, dear,' she breathed.

'You will leave at once!'

'I won't, you know.' She curled up on the bed, offering him a long length of leg. 'What are you going to do? Call out the guard?'

'I – ' Ebbs stopped. He wondered what the devil he would do.

She laughed. 'Give me a light, sweetie.'

Ebbs blew his nose urgently. With professional quickness of thought in emergency he decided that tact was the only lever likely to ease her off his bed. He obediently picked up a matchbox from the dressing-table, and struck a light. She held his wrist tightly as he lit her cigarette, and asked, 'How about a little drink?'

'Haven't you had enough already?'

She looked at him coyly. 'It's my birthday.'

'Of course you can have a drink,' Ebbs said, with a flash of cunning. 'They're all in the day-cabin.'

'Luring the cat with a saucer of milk? She laughed again. 'Bring one in *here*, darling. It's ever so much cosier.'

Ebbs exploded in a flash of irritation. 'But damn it –!'

'Sssssh!' She put her finger to her lips. 'Aren't you *noisy*, darling. You don't want everyone on board to hear you, surely? Now just get me a little drink like the sweet angel you are. Then I'll go away.'

'You really will?'

'Of *course* I will, darling.'

'You can have mine if you like.' He gave her the glass, and she patted the bed-cover.

'Come and sit down, and we'll have a little chat. Come *on*, darling!' she insisted. 'I'll go in a minute.'

Ebbs sat down on the bed like a man getting into an over-hot bath.

'Aren't you shy!' she coaxed. 'Haven't you ever had any girlfriends?'

'I must ask you to remember my position, madam,' Ebbs began carefully. He desperately decided on an appeal of reason and better nature. 'I am the Captain of this ship, and expected to set a good example to my officers – also, I might add, to my passengers. The slightest breath of scandal would be disastrous to my authority. And possibly to my job. That is why I really must ask you – if you have any kindness and consideration at all – to leave my cabin at the earliest possible moment.'

'What's this?' she asked, picking up a brass cup clipped over the bunk.

'For God's sake, put that down!' Ebbs threw out his arm to grab it and spilt the whisky. The *Charlemagne*, like other electrified ships, still preserved on the bridge reliable apparatus like a telescope and the Captain's voice-pipe. Mrs Porteous unstoppered the short tube leading to the wheelhouse above, and gave a short blast on its commanding whistle.

'Put it down!' Ebbs hissed. He tried to clap his hand over it, but she giggled and held it against the top of her dress. As she grasped the pipe she suddenly let go and powerfully embraced him instead. He sealed the mouthpiece with his damp palm, and she began spraying his face with uninhibited kisses.

'Let go!' Ebbs muttered in terror. 'For God's sake, let me go!' Already he had heard the hasty clatter on the bridge ladder; a knock came immediately at his day-cabin door.

'Don't make a sound!' he commanded fiercely. He closed the night-cabin door, remembered to wipe his face with a handkerchief, and opened the door beyond. Brickwood, standing at attention outside, gave a stiff salute.

'Is anything wrong, sir?'

'Er – no, Mr Brickwood. Nothing…nothing's wrong at all…'

'I thought you called on the voice-pipe, sir?'

'Some bad dream, Mr Brickwood,' Ebbs said breathlessly. 'Calling out in the sleep, you know. Well-known failing of mine. Very distressing. Sorry I disturbed the bridge.'

'You were asleep, sir?' Brickwood looked puzzled. Ebbs glanced down at his stiff shirt-front and trousers.

'Dozed off on my bunk, I suppose. Tiring day. Thank you, Mr Brickwood. Very pleased to see you keeping such a good watch.'

Brickwood saluted again. 'Good night, sir.'

'Good night, Mr Brickwood.'

Ebbs shut the door and leaned for a second against the bulkhead inside. Then he sprang for the inner door determinedly.

'Mrs Porteous…!' he began forcefully. He stopped. She had taken her dress off.

'What are you doing?' he demanded. 'Are you mad? Are you determined to ruin me? Have you no sense of shame? Can't you go elsewhere?'

'Shhhhh!' she said. 'Or I'll scream – through this.'

'Leave that voice-pipe alone, I pray you!' Ebbs cried fervently.

RICHARD GORDON

'Come and sit down beside me, then, sweetie. We haven't finished our little chat, have we?'

'Have you no thought for your husband?' said Ebbs feebly.

'Of course, darling – why don't you relax a little?' A plump naked arm reached out for him.

'This is impossible!' he cried. 'Absolutely impossible! I give you exactly two minutes to leave this cabin.'

'But you can't turn a girl out without her dress on, can you sweet?'

'*With* your dress on!'

'No, sweetie,' she said firmly. 'Here I am – and here I stay.'

'You are not, madam, you are not!'

'Don't madam me, dear, please.'

'Go!' he pointed to the door.

She began taking off her brassière.

Ebbs arrived breathlessly on the bridge. He immediately grabbed the top of the voice-pipe.

'Anything wrong, sir?' Brickwood asked, saluting brilliantly and trying to look unconcerned.

'I thought I'd come up for a little fresh air, Mr Brickwood.'

'Oh, I see, sir.'

'Please carry on with your watch. Pay no attention to me at all.'

'Very good, sir. But aren't you a little cold, sir? You're hardly – fully dressed, sir.'

'I was rather hot in my mess-jacket. Touch of the fever, possibly. I'll see the Doctor in the morning.'

'I'm sorry, sir. You certainly don't look very well, sir.'

'Thank you, Mr Brickwood. Er – if you wish you may remove your own jacket. The Regulation – possibly relaxed… Carry on with the watch. I'll stay here.'

'Very good, sir.'

As Brickwood turned away the first lines of *I Can't Give You Anything but Love* came up the voice-pipe. Ebbs stuck his elbow on it.

'I beg your pardon, sir?' Brickwood's eyebrows were raised to his cap-peak.

'Nothing, Mr Brickwood. I was merely singing to myself.'

'Yes, sir.'

Brickwood went out to the wing of the bridge and leaned thoughtfully over the starboard light. He wondered if he should call out the Doctor straight away and have Ebbs overpowered by the Quartermasters before he could do serious harm, or wait until daylight when his chances of escaping to terrorise the ship would be lessened. He edged towards a marline-spike by the rail and thoughtfully slipped it up his sleeve. Ebbs was standing in the wheelhouse with an appearance of deep misery, staring at the top of the voice-pipe as if he expected a dangerous snake to crawl out. He was still there when the watch changed at four. At six he made his way nervously to his cabin, and to his immeasurable relief found that Mrs Porteous had gone.

11

Shawe-Wilson came to Ebbs' cabin the next morning prepared to fight for his job. With daylight he saw bitterly that Ebbs was right. Although Captain Buckle had smiled at cautious wenching by his officers, a report that the Chief Officer had been caught making love to the Company's passengers on the boat-deck would stand out ruinously from the papers on McWhirrey's desk. He had prepared his ditches carefully while shaving: first, he thought it was allowed; second, he was doing his duty by encouraging the social life of the ship; third, the poor girl was lonely; fourth, he loved her; fifth, the lapse would never occur again, if he had the continued honour of serving under Ebbs' command; last, it wasn't him at all, but the Second Engineer.

He knocked on Ebbs' door, saluted, slipped his cap smartly under his arm, and entered.

Ebbs looked up. He was red-eyed and pale, sitting bleakly over the unaccustomed remains of his breakfast.

'You sent for me, sir.'

'Did I?'

'Yes, sir.' Shawe-Wilson looked surprised. 'Last night. On the bridge.'

Ebbs gazed sorrowfully at the toast-rack. 'I should have expected from you, Mr Shawe-Wilson,' he said with more admiration than censure, 'a little greater discretion. Good morning.'

Shawe-Wilson stared at him.

'That is all,' Ebbs said, waving him away.

'Yes, sir. Thank you, sir. Good morning, sir.' He replaced his cap, saluted absently and stumbled from the cabin.

Outside, he lit a cigarette. He had knocked on the door steeling himself for any punishment up to instant dismissal, and Ebbs had treated him less severely than if he had lost the chartroom rubber or blotted the log book. He frowned down the alleyway. As he felt he could reliably discount feelings of charity, he wondered what had compelled his Captain to change his mind.

Brickwood's head appeared round his cabin door.

'Chief!' he hissed. 'Have you seen the Old Man?'

'I've just been in with him. Why?'

'Is he foaming at the mouth?' Brickwood tapped his forehead. 'He's crackers.'

'Oh, I know that,' Shawe-Wilson said absently. He paced thoughtfully towards his own cabin, his mind beginning to run along familiar paths. But first he had to restore his self-esteem, so he went to order the quartermasters to clean out the lifeboats.

Ebbs continued to sit motionless over his dead breakfast, wondering what his reputation was in the ship. He ardently hoped the dawn had been sufficiently tinged with shame to silence Mrs Porteous; if he could now persuade Brickwood that he had been in the grip of some spasmodic fever the recent irregularities in his cabin might stay unsuspected. For a moment he considered sending for the ship's Doctor to fortify his story with the rumour of a consultation, or even turning in and falsifying a roaring temperature under the bathroom tap.

He looked up. Burtweed was standing beside him with a tray.

'Yes, Burtweed?' he asked disinterestedly.

'I beg your pardon, sir. But if you would kindly tell me the name of the lady who owns the bracelet, I could slip it back in her cabin.'

Ebbs glanced at the thick gold clasp-bracelet in the middle of the tray.

'How on earth should I know?' he asked peevishly. 'Put it with the other bric-a-brac left over from the party. The owner will no doubt come and claim it soon enough.'

Burtweed coughed. 'Pardon, sir. I discovered this one in your night-cabin, sir.'

Ebbs licked his lips. 'It possibly moved in there, Burtweed.'

'Possibly, sir.'

Ebbs saw on the tray his whisky glass, thickly bitten with lipstick, and the accusing red-stained stub of a cigarette.

'With great respect, sir,' Burtweed went on, 'it might be more discreet for me to return this one personal.'

Ebbs stood up. He opened his cabin door, looked outside, carefully closed it, and began striding up and down with his hands behind his back.

'Burtweed,' he said resolutely, 'you have been Tiger to several Captains… '

'Not one of which I've regretted, sir.'

'Quite. You have no doubt observed enough to appreciate the difficulties that beset them. I feel entitled, therefore, to take a somewhat unusual course. I am going to confide in you, Burtweed. It won't go any further?' he asked in sudden alarm.

'Oh, no, sir!' Burtweed was shocked. 'Across my heart, sir,' he added, slapping his left chest heartily.

'Good. Well, you are perfectly correct. There was a woman in my cabin last night.'

'Congratulations, sir.'

'It is not a cause for congratulation, Burtweed. The visitor came unasked, and left – ah, unsatisfied.'

'I see, sir.'

'Does it mean,' Ebbs asked with increasing warmth, 'that I am to be the target of every designing woman on board? I, of all people – whose very job depends on keeping my reputation above reproach? Does every woman who wants a bedfellow at sea make for the Captain? Don't they ever have a go at the Chief Engineer?'

'Bless us, yes, sir!' Burtweed said. 'It's always the Captain. He's the prize pippin of the lot, if you'll excuse the term, sir.'

'But isn't there anything I can do about it? Why, it's ludicrous! How can I be expected to discipline my officers if they think I lead the life of a – libertine?'

'Captain Buckle, sir, set great store by his woodwork. He said no woman could get romantic in the same room as a lathe.'

There was silence, as Ebbs sat down and stared anxiously through the porthole.

'Might I ask, sir,' Burtweed said, 'if you are blessed with a good woman and little ones?'

'No, Burtweed, I am not.'

'Nor I, sir. But such might offer you some protection.'

'Burtweed, I can hardly marry and raise a family in a single voyage,' Ebbs said crossly.

'I don't mean in the flesh, sir,' Burtweed explained. 'If you'll pardon the expression. There's a good many of the lads down below who invent the encumbrances, sir. Very useful for them playing about with the girls on the coast. Why, half the ship is pretending to the Aussie girls they're married to keep 'em off, and the other half is pretending they ain't to egg 'em on.'

Ebbs grunted.

Burtweed fumbled beneath his white jacket. 'With great respect, sir, I've a photo here of my niece in South America and her two nippers. If you like, sir, you can have a loan of it till the end of the voyage. You could stick it on your desk, sir, to keep the flies off as it were.'

He handed Ebbs a cracked and dog-eared photograph. The Burtweed great-nephews had an odd appearance, through their eyes seeming nearer their ears than to each other. The picture was in colour, bringing out savagely the blonde hair and lilac dress of the mother, and giving one child the look of a blue baby and the other of having florid scarlet fever.

Ebbs laid the card against his pokerwork pipe-rack. 'I appreciate your kindness, Burtweed,' he said. 'I only trust it will prove a powerful enough deterrent. In any case I shall in future keep my cabin locked in the evenings. Now please remove that finery from my sight. You can return it to Cabin A25. I may trust you to do so without attracting attention?'

'Not a mortal soul, sir,' Burtweed assured him gravely. 'You'd be surprised at some of the things I've had to return for Captains in my time.'

And now, said Ebbs to himself, I shall have to start steeling myself for lunch.

But Mrs Porteous had the good grace to develop a headache.

12

The *Charlemagne* began to approach the hot Egyptian corner of the Mediterranean at Suez and run among the homeward-bound ships scattering north of the Canal. This traffic obliged Ebbs to take personal command again to the bridge, and he was grateful for an official excuse to stay away from his passengers and avoid the eye of Mrs Porteous. He appeared in a heavy greatcoat and two mufflers, demanded that all the wheelhouse doors and scuttles should be shut, and continually sneezed and chewed formalin throat lozenges to impress his officers that he was recovering from some violent infection.

The following afternoon the ship slowed and slipped into the grey oily water between the long thin arms of the Suez breakwaters. Her anchors fell with stately splashes into the Canal, launches snatched at her ropes, and she was moored between a pair of buoys at the tail of a long queue of ships. Port Said swept away to starboard, equally and inseparably historical and fabulous, the grating hinge between East and West durably polished up by Kipling. When McWhirrey's steamers had first shuttled sahibs and soldiers between Plymouth and Bombay in the reassuring leathery gloom of good London clubs, a Pole Star ship with blackened hatches at the coaling berth was as much a part of the Port Said scene as the sand and newly risen minarets. Here the chilly old gentlemen in topcoats who had miserably sipped their Bovril on the rainy Channel decks strode majestically in their accustomed whites and called imperiously for burra pegs, and the social divisions of British India stood out like the ship's brasswork in the intensifying sun. When the *Charlemagne* had sailed sluggishly below the statue of sad de Lesseps pointing the way to India and sighted the rich domes of the Moorish Custom House, her passengers gathered on deck as excitedly as their Victorian predecessors for their first glimpse of the East. They strained their eyes across the strange architecture for the herald call of Islam, already visible in large red script on a high wall by the Simon Artz Bazaar. As the ship approached the writing grew, clarified, and became readable: *Coco-Cola* it said.

Ebbs left the bridge as soon as the moorings were secure, and found the desk in his cabin thickly covered with envelopes. He immediately opened one from McWhirrey.

Dear Captain (it said)

Do I have to tell each of our Captains, every voyage, of the undesirability of courting publicity like film actresses? I will stress again the importance of your reading Company Regulations, Para. 1005, which expressly forbids interviews with newspaper reporters without prior consent of the Company. The grossest misrepresentations can occur. As you seem determined to thrust your new command on the public eye, I will remind you of the conditions under which you hold it.

Yours, etc.

Angus McWhirrey

Ebbs scratched his head in bewilderment. Interviews with newspaper reporters? He was old-fashioned enough for a journalist to affect him like a pin in a live winkle. In a daze, he opened the next letter, from his sister.

Dear Billy (she said)

So you're famous at last! Mr Trouneer next door showed me the cutting from the paper by Willy Boast. It's called 'England's Other Captain by Radio'. He writes all about that awful gale you were lucky to survive, and how you took the ship through without turning a hair (he says a Bradman facing elemental bowlers). I should think Sir Angus would be very pleased to see that! He also puts a lot about dinner at your table, and says you are a nautical diplomat and witty. I can't get that red stain off your whites, it must be fruit juice. You must be careful at meals, you always were a messy eater. Wrap up well at night, it is very treacherous and you have a weak chest. Don't forget to take your opening medicine on Fridays.

Your loving sister,
Maria

With a sigh, Ebbs let the two letters flutter on to his desk. This was too much even for anger. After a week's struggle against bullies, bickerers, importunate adolescents, and mature nymphomaniacs, his ruin had been completed by an oaf who had been conscious only of the opening and shutting of the ship's bar since leaving London.

'Hallo, hallo, hallo!' came a hearty voice from the cabin door. Ebbs looked up slowly. It was Berris, the Company's Port Said agent, a cheerful Londoner whom he had detested for several years. 'Well, if it isn't old Ebbs, eh?' the man went on, throwing his hat on the sofa. 'And what a change of scenery, if I may say so! When I got the cable from London you could have knocked me for six – I bet old Ebbs is kicking himself for taking it on, I said. Why, he's far too old a dog to learn new tricks, I said. Eh?' He poked Ebbs in the ribs. 'How do you like your floating gin-palace?'

'All ships are the same,' said Ebbs. But the certainty had been crushed from his voice.

'Mind if I help myself to a peg? This is a change from the old bottle in the boot locker, I will say.' He poured himself half a tumbler of whisky. 'The *Luther*'ll be through here in a couple of weeks – how shall I tell your old crew you're getting on?'

'If I know my old crew,' Ebbs said gloomily, turning to the rest of his mail, 'they will have already decided how I am getting on.'

'I said to the wife,' the Agent continued, settling with his drink on a corner of the desk. '"I bet old Ebbs finds out a thing or two." I was joking, mind. I said, "I can just see him now, sitting there at dinner, all dressed up like a little dog's breakfast and looking like when one of the old *Luther's* plates had sprung again." Didn't we laugh!' He roared for some moments at the recollection. '"I bet that he tried to tell them a funny story," I said.'

He wiped his eyes. "'And I bet – I bet it flops!'" He put down his glass and held his sides. 'We were only having a bit of fun, mind. "And I reckon he'll have a hell of a time with half the women on board after him," I said. Gawd! We laughed for hours! But the funniest thing of the lot – '

'Yes, Mr Brickwood?' Ebbs interrupted.

'A passenger is creating a disturbance by the accommodation ladder, sir.'

'A passenger? Which one?'

'Brigadier Broster, sir. He doesn't see why he shouldn't be allowed ashore.'

'Tell him cholera is raging,' Ebbs said. 'Also that the Egyptians have declared war. Now Mr Berris, we shall attend exclusively to the business of the ship.'

The *Charlemagne's* passengers, kept on board because she was pausing only a few hours before moving down the Canal in the evening convoy, soon tired of their new surroundings like young children at the Zoo. They wandered uncertainly round the decks trying to recapture their mid-ocean enthusiasm for quoits and shuffle-board, became increasingly bad-tempered, and finally leaned on the rails striking bargains with the swarming bum-boat men, a pastime as extravagant as playing on fruit-machines. The only contented soul on board was Burtweed. The *Charlemagne's* environment never troubled him. As he rarely went ashore and it was always hot down below, it made no difference to the Tiger whether she lay in London, Port Said, or Sydney. In the cheerless cabin at water level which he shared with five other stewards he found peace. At sea, he always held himself ready to jump to the Captain's attendance, but in port he suspended his service for a quiet hour to enjoy the only dissipation of his life. He took off his white jacket and his sharply-creased serge trousers, and hung them carefully on a coat-hanger above his bunk. This left him in the woollen combinations he wore conscientiously in cool latitudes to seal in the health and sunshine of the tropics. From a marbled brown tin trunk below his bunk he drew a large enamel basin, which he took to the steward's mess-room and filled with steaming water. Back in

81

his cabin, he carefully removed his shoes and socks, drew a new packet of aromatic salts from his trunk, tipped the lot into the water, and rapturously bathed his feet. Burtweed suffered badly from the feet, and at sea massaged them, anointed them with a green oil sold only by a barber in Dock Street, and daily buttressed his shoes with pads of cotton wool. But only in port, when the Captain's needs were more predictable and the mechanics of foot-bathing simpler, did he allow himself the extreme sensuality that he anticipated across the ocean as longingly as the more usual shoregoing pleasures of his shipmates.

It was soon dark, and the regulation Canal searchlight was hoisted to the bows, manned by a crew of unidentifiable nationalities. Shortly afterwards the *Charlemagne* got under way in a procession of tankers balanced on the water like celluloid ducks, sailing empty to Basra and Kuwait. Ebbs surrendered the wheelhouse to the Canal Company's pilot, a Frenchman who leant against the chartroom door smoking *Gitanes* and uttering nothing all night except his helm orders and demands for hot coffee. At daybreak the ship found herself still moving between unlimited banks of greyish sand, and the passengers were already up and scattered thinly on the decks as the convoy debouched abruptly between the bright houses of Port Taufiq into the sea. The Pole Star Company expected no delay: pilot, searchlight, and shore gang were dropped into breathless launches hurrying against the *Charlemagne's* flanks, and immediately Ebbs ordered the engine-room telegraphs to ring Full Ahead. Then he inspected the bridge thermometer and announced:

'Going to be a scorcher today, Mr Brickwood.'

'I wouldn't be surprised, sir.'

'We shall have rig of the day all white, then. Kindly present my compliments to Mr Shawe-Wilson and tell him to see that all heads of departments are informed before breakfast.'

'Aye aye, sir.'

'Let us hope,' Ebbs said, gazing anxiously aft along the freshly-swabbed passenger decks, 'that the brighter sunshine promises a brighter voyage.'

Within an hour the ship's company appeared in their stiff unsweated white uniforms, and the passengers began to fumble for their sunglasses and peel away the last of their European coverings. Swiftly drawing away from her companions in the convoy, with the bleak African cliffs on one side and the faint Biblical cone of Sinai on the other, the *Charlemagne* bit into the fervid Red Sea and Ebbs' troubles really began.

13

In a patch of shade at the after end of the boat deck Annette sat with her latest fiancé, a thin sad young man in spectacles going out to lecture in Botany at Sydney University. They occupied a pair of hot steamer chairs, and each sipped a John Collins which was being rapidly diluted by the melting ice. Annette wore a smart red swimsuit, and he only an old pair of khaki shorts rolled up his thighs. Their skins were scarlet, and as fragile as the scales of freshly-boiled salmon.

'This *heat*!' Annette groaned.

'The famous Red Sea,' he said.

'But I never thought it would be so beastly hot as *this*! If there isn't a breeze soon I'll go *mad*. Stark staring raving.'

'People go mad in these latitudes pretty often,' he told her thoughtfully. 'It's renowned for it.'

On the deck below a dozen couples splashed in the captive square of water in the swimming-pool. Beyond, the wake frothed away into the empty blue sea, which ran towards the unbroken sky to seal the ship in a steamy envelope.

'How long till lunch?' pouted Annette.

Looking at his watch was the effort of shifting a grand piano. 'Half an hour.'

'I never thought meals could be so beastly important. It's like being ill in bed.'

As he said nothing, she yawned. 'How bored I am! Can't we have another drink?'

He raised his sunglasses briefly. 'Can't see the deck steward.'

They both fell silent, hypnotised by the heat.

'Talk to me,' she demanded.

With a sigh he looked round for a subject and picked up one of the Pole Star Line folders that were distributed thickly through the ship. ' "Your ticket is a token for sunshine and service," ' he read aloud. ' "Three weeks of luxury and a lifetime of memories! The radiance of a tropical morning at sea greets you through your porthole when you awaken. The sun caresses you through a day of luxurious idleness. At night, the soft light of the tropical moon and the gentle pitter-patter of the waves lull you to sleep on the deep…" ' He let the leaflet drop on the deck and groaned.

'I wish I'd gone by air,' she said.

'So do I.'

'How long is it now till lunch?'

'Twenty-five minutes.'

She tinkled the last specks of ice round her glass. 'How beastly!'

'Don't look up,' he said urgently. 'Here comes the Captain.'

'Oh, gosh! If he starts being sociable I shall go *mad.*'

'Let's pretend we're asleep.'

'Look at his knees,' she whispered. 'Men like that shouldn't be allowed to wear shorts.'

It was Ebbs' social half-hour. When the ship had left Suez he saw it clearly his duty to make wider acquaintance with his passengers, and had asked Burtweed's advice how to set about it. 'One can hardly intrude into private conversations,' he explained. 'But otherwise they seem to take very little notice of me. Why,' he went on indignantly, 'I stood by the swimming bath for twenty minutes this morning, and my only acknowledgement was a severe splashing from one of those young women gymnasts. I quite believe on purpose.'

'If I may suggest, sir,' Burtweed said kindly. 'You should make your appearances regular. Like the stewards with the beef tea and ice creams.'

'You think that would help?'

'Oh, yes, sir. The passengers know you're coming then, and don't wonder if you're after them for misbehaving, or to take round the plate on Sunday or run the race meeting, sir.

'I see.' Ebbs said doubtfully. 'Captain Buckle was sociable by the clock, I take it?'

'Bless us, yes, sir. Every day at half past twelve regular he'd say, "Give us me hat, Burtweed, I'm off to butter up these bloody bastards what pays my rent." With respect, sir.'

Thereafter at twelve-thirty punctually Ebbs stepped from his cabin and toured the boat-deck with the steely joviality of an election candidate. But he found his approach had the effect of a deck-chair attendant on a promenade: the passengers either scuttled away, buried their heads in their books like ostriches, or instantly sank into a deep sleep.

Continuing hopefully round the deck past Annette, Ebbs came upon Canon Swingle, sitting in correct and decent linen reading a book.

'Well, Canon!' he said cheerfully. 'Not so cold today, eh?'

The Canon thought deeply, and after a while said, 'No. Not so cold today, Captain.'

Ebbs glanced towards the glassy water. 'Rough sea,' he ventured.

After several seconds' careful search to the horizon the Canon declared: 'Mercifully calm.'

'Well,' Ebbs said. He saluted. 'Well,' he said again.

Canon Swingle nodded, and returned to the place he was keeping with his finger on the page.

The next target for his politeness was Mrs Lomax, round the corner of the ship's upper-works.

'Good morning, madam! Enjoying the balmy breezes of the sea?'

A look of intense concern came on her face, and she began fumbling with her hearing-aid.

'Just a minute, Captain,' she said nervously.

'Don't worry, don't worry!' Ebbs shouted. 'I merely inquired if you were enjoying the balmy breezes of the sea?'

'What's that, Captain?' she asked. She imagined he was telling her to swim for her life.

'I merely said, "Are you enjoying the balmy breezes of the sea?"' Ebbs roared. Two girls, apparently in a coma in neighbouring deck-chairs, broke into sniggers.

'Oh, the balmy breezes? Yes, yes!' Mrs Lomax said in relief, as she found the switch. 'Oh, yes, very much, thank you, Captain.'

'And how are you today?' Ebbs continued, so that most of the deck could hear.

'Very poorly. Very poorly indeed.'

'But you look very well, madam!' he shouted encouragingly.

'My looks belie me. They always have. I've been poorly for years. For years and years.' She sighed. 'Now I have nothing to look forward to except to be reunited with my dear husband.'

'Yes,' Ebbs roared. 'He will be waiting with a bunch of flowers on the quay at Fremantle, I'll be bound!'

'He has been dead for several years,' she said and loudly burst into tears.

Ebbs stumbled backwards in embarrassment, tripped against the foot of a *chaise-longue,* knocked over a pile of ice-cream plates, and hid himself behind the fanhouse.

'Captain!' boomed a voice immediately behind him.

He shut his eyes.

'I'd like a few words with you, Captain.'

Broster was sitting at ease in a steamer-chair, in a pair of white ducks, a yachting cap, an MCC tie, and a pair of fearsome sunglasses. At his side were conveniently arranged a glass of iced lager, several old copies of the *Financial Times,* a box of cigars, a bottle of bicarbonate, a pair of binoculars in case of passing ships, a fly swat, a pile of detective stories, and a small private handbell for summoning the deck steward.

'I must get up to the bridge – '

'I won't keep you a minute. I am explaining to Commander Barker here what to do with the Royal Navy.'

'Got to go and write some letters,' Commander Barker announced, slipping off his chair and disappearing down a handy companionway.

'My breakfast egg,' Brigadier Broster declared, as if issuing a challenge, 'was cold this morning. I wouldn't complain in the ordinary way – I'm not the complaining type. I'm just an ordinary fare-paying passenger. But it was cold yesterday morning. And the morning before. And tomorrow no doubt it will be cold as well.'

'I'll speak to the Purser about it.'

'Furthermore, there's some infernal thing that goes drum-drum-drum all night in my cabin. Don't know what it is, but get it fixed. It may interest you to know that I haven't had my eyes shut more than half an hour since I left home.'

'I'll see the Chief Engineer immediately.'

'And the ship's water. Where did you get the ship's water, Captain?'

'It was freshly taken on in Port Said, sir.'

'Cholera, by God!' Broster exclaimed. 'I suppose you had it tested?'

Ebbs suddenly wondered whether he should have ordered someone to analyse it.

'Well, sir, I am hardly responsible – '

'Then it's cholera. No doubt about it. I have had a looseness of the bowels since Suez. It'll be round the ship like wildfire, and you'll be damn lucky, I should say, if you sailed into Aden with more than half your passengers still alive. Manslaughter, Captain! Murder, possibly. However, you are responsible for your own folly.' He folded his arms, as if determined to die on the spot out of spite. 'Also,' he added, 'there are weasels in the bread.'

'If you really mean weasels I'll have them destroyed. But now I really must ask you to let me proceed to the bridge. I have to give my orders. Among other things, about your cabin and your eggs.'

'Well, don't forget, Captain.' Broster shook his finger. 'I may be simply an ordinary passenger – but I have my duty to the Line. I might tell you I shall be writing to Sir Angus very fully from Aden. Very fully indeed.'

'I hope,' Ebbs said earnestly, 'that you will then have no cause for complaint.'

'We shall see, Captain. We shall see. Ah, Father Hennessy,' he exclaimed, as a little fat man in tennis flannels tried to sneak behind Ebbs to the companionway. 'Just a minute, will you? I'd like to go on giving you my views on the Roman Catholic Church.'

Ebbs escaped to the forward part of the boat-deck in a mood of deepening pessimism. He had set out with a bunch of conversational flowers, and they had withered in his hand. The interview with Broster was disturbing, and feeling the need to compose his thoughts he dodged under a rope that temporarily separated a small square of the deck for repainting. As it was empty for the crew's dinner hour he warily found a dry stretch of rail and leaned on it alone. At Aden the voyage would be half over. On the credit side, he was still in command of the ship, Mrs Porteous had apparently been shamed into silence, Shawe-Wilson now did no work at all but at least kept out of his way, and though his officers thought he was insane, they had no suspicion that he had been on the same bed as one of his passengers. But if the ship's mailbags went over the side in Aden stuffed with letters of complaint... The stark hull of the *Martin Luther* shimmered on the horizon like the *Flying Dutchman*.

A light and hesitant jerk came on his shirt-sleeve. He looked round in surprise. A small straw-haired, large-eyed female child was looking up at him.

'Hello,' Ebbs said. He had noticed bands of children roaming the decks like wild Dartmoor ponies, but he was too shy a man to greet them. 'What, all alone?' he asked, impulsively.

She nodded solemnly.

A small child renounced by her friends, lonely and misunderstood, immediately ignited in him a glow of sympathy.

'And what's your name, little girl?' he inquired benevolently.

'Priscilla,' she said firmly.

'Now that's a very pretty name, isn't it?'

'No,' she declared. '*I* don't think it's pretty. I think it's borjewahs.'

'Where are your Mummy and Daddy?'

'In the bar.'

'And where are all your little friends?'

'I find them rather tejus,' she announced.

'How old are you?' Ebbs asked suspiciously. He had small experience of children, and wondered for a moment if he might be talking to some female dwarf.

'Nine. How old are you?'

'That doesn't matter.'

She began to look at him with growing interest. '*Who* are you?' she asked.

'I'm the Captain.'

'And what do you do?'

'I do lots of things.'

'What sort of things?'

'Well – things like finding out where the ship's going, and so forth.'

'How do you do that?'

'It would take far too long to explain, my dear young lady,' he said. He reached out a hand and patted her gingerly on the head, as if she were a large strange dog.

'If you're the Captain, are you still cold?' she asked.

'Cold? My dear girl, I assure you I am at the moment extremely hot.'

'No you're not. I heard one of the ladies say so. She said, the Captain's as frigid as a block of ice.'

'What! And where may I ask, did you hear that?'

'This morning. I was in the loo.'

'Now look here, my girl,' Ebbs said sternly. 'It is very naughty indeed to go round repeating things you hear in – in places.' He wagged his finger strongly in her face. 'Do you understand that? You must on no account tell it to anyone else. I am the Captain, and I can have little girls thrown to the sharks if I like,' he continued, sincerely wishing he could.

She dropped her eyes shamefully, and two tears spilt on to her cheeks. Ebbs immediately felt remorse.

'Dear me, dear me! Don't cry, little girl,' he said. She continued to sob, so he felt in his pocket for the half-crown he was saving for bingo. There you are – now go and buy yourself some sweeties at the barber's shop.'

'Thank you,' she said demurely, grabbing the money with both hands.

Ebbs smiled at her again, and awarded her another amiable tap. How could she be blamed for repeating unintelligible gossip? He felt that his faith in humanity had been restored a little by her touching innocence.

'Run along, Priscilla,' he said gently. 'Bye, bye!' He turned towards his cabin.

Something hit him sharply between the shoulder-blades. A ball of cotton waste, soaked through in the bos'n's red lead, dropped with a splash on the deck.

'You little devil!' Ebbs roared.

'Captain's frigid, Captain's frigid, Captain's frigid!' she chanted excitedly, dodging among the passengers like a squeaking bat.

Ebbs started after her, but stopped hopelessly. 'Women!' he said. He went into his quarters and slammed the door. The red lead was beginning to soak through to his back. He had only another clean shirt to last until Aden. And at lunch Broster was bound to start talking about his bowels.

14

In the afternoon it became hotter.

By now the passengers' nerves were as sensitive as their skins. They felt they had been living in the *Charlemagne* since birth and had as little chance of escaping from her alive as the complement in *Outward Bound*. Every day had become the same – too long to live and too short to remember. Their lives were marched wearily between the milestones of their meals, with encouragement from the lesser posts of morning ices, afternoon tea, and sandwich supper. Although the ship's gossips still conjured each smile across the shuffleboard and every creaking cabin in the night into a new romance, the passionate attachments of the Mediterranean had begun to smoulder and die, and the lifelong friendships north of Suez were hourly destroyed by such momentous trifles as using the hair-dryer out of turn or grabbing someone else's favourite pastry. Deck-tennis was played with Wimbledon acrimony, the bridge players now conversed only in bids, and the drinkers alone remained happy as they floated along in their soft protective pink cocoons of alcohol.

Then at dinner the air-conditioning broke down.

The *Charlemagne's* saloon had been designed in obedience to her ventilating system, and was as tightly sealed as a diving-helmet. The passengers sweated richly at the tables, picking their way through the ship's inflexibly English menu of roast beef and Yorkshire pudding. Ebbs felt his shirt-front sagging like a sheet of wet blotting-paper, as he sat in silence with his eyes fixed glassily on the fruit-garnished centre-piece. Even the bickering Cokes were stilled by the heat, and Mrs Porteous spoke solely to ask Ebbs for the salt and pepper in tones suggesting they were objects of the closest intimacy between them. There was only Brigadier Broster to play the conversation like a solo on the tuba.

'In England,' he said loudly in the direction of Bill Coke, 'we live in large houses. Often very old houses. With picture galleries.' He ate a roast potato. 'I have a very large picture gallery in my house. It is worth many hundred thousands of pounds, I believe. Last year I had a man down to renovate my pictures. Clean them up, you know. Steward! Take back this horseradish. And when I got home from my office,' he continued, 'I found my wife very excited. She becomes excited very easily. "R B," she said. "The man has found a Van Dyck in the gallery." "Very good," I said. "I will go and see if he's right. But after dinner." In England we do not care to get excited, and to spoil our dinners. So we had dinner – smoked trout, I remember, followed by game pie. We had a bottle of some ordinary Burgundy. After dinner we took a candle and I had the butler bring a pair of steps. We looked for the Van Dyck – it was somewhere near the roof, in the darkness. Hadn't noticed it. I inspected it, and I said to my wife, "My dear," I said, "it *is* a Van Dyck." But it wasn't a very *good* Van Dyck. So we left it where it was.'

He stopped, and began to munch his salad noisily.

'What do you think of that?' he demanded.

'I don't blame you,' Bill Coke said absently, wiping his head and neck with a yellow handkerchief. 'Those bloody Dutch liqueurs never did agree with me.'

The next morning Ebbs woke up covered with spots.

'It was the fish, sir,' Burtweed declared. 'I told the chef it was off.'

'I don't care what it was,' he said. 'It's damnably uncomfortable.'

'Shall I send for the Doctor, sir?'

'No, no!' Ebbs always associated the medical profession with his sister. 'It'll probably disappear during the day.'

He sat down for breakfast, scratching himself vigorously.

'With great respect, sir, perhaps you should rub yourself with vinegar. Over the exposed parts. If you'll pardon the expression, sir.'

Ebbs grunted.

'There was one poor gentleman I was Tiger to,' Burtweed continued, tenderly reminiscent. 'Captain Pick it was, sir, in the old *Augustus*. He came out in spots all over on the Friday, sir – I remember it was Friday particular, because it was Good Friday – and by Easter Monday he was dead, sir.'

'Burtweed,' Ebbs said, waving a knife at him. 'Go away.'

'I meant no offence, sir.'

'Get out!'

'Yes, sir. Shall I tell the religious gentlemen to wait, sir?'

'What religious gentlemen?'

'They've been outside the door, since seven-thirty, sir.'

Six parsons came into the cabin, all looking disagreeable.

'Well?' Ebbs snapped, wondering what could be the cause of the visitation. Suddenly remembering that he was addressing the Company's passengers, he added as amiably as possible, 'and what can I do for you, please?'

Canon Swingle cleared his throat and stood on one foot. 'Captain,' he said. 'I fear a separation – indeed, a divorce – is necessary. I speak myself as one already removed from the seat of the trouble, but the table occupied by my colleagues in the saloon clearly can no longer continue as it is.' He lowered his eyes. 'Mr Toddy here threw a plate of cornflakes at Mr McBride this morning.'

'Just look at my stock!' exclaimed McBride, opening his linen jacket. 'Ruined!'

'But what on earth did you want to do a thing like that for?' Ebbs asked, still scratching himself.

'He threw his puffed rice at me first!' said Toddy hotly. He was a pale, congenitally curatish young man.

'Mr Toddy,' McBride said. 'You are not only no gentleman, but you are also a callous murderer of the truth.'

'Mr McBride, it is no use trying to cover yourself with bombast. Father Hennessy saw you do it.'

'Mr Toddy, I tell you I never did any such thing. Besides, you have a disgusting habit of mashing up your cornflakes with marmalade – '

'No worse than your quite nauseating practice of sticking bits of bread in your egg.'

McBride clenched his fists. 'Mr Toddy, I intend to give you a good hiding.'

'Mr McBride, please go ahead and try.'

'Gentlemen, gentlemen!' Ebbs cried, as Canon Swingle and the others intervened to prevent the deputation turning into a free fight. 'I would hardly have expected such behaviour. Really! Please remember yourselves. Of course, I can rearrange the saloon seating if strictly necessary, but it will cause considerable trouble to the ship...'

'I would not sit with Mr McBride to eat my last crust!' Toddy said shrilly.

'I may say I am quite content in my new place,' Canon Swingle murmured. 'Quite content.'

Ebbs called Prittlewell on the ship's phone as soon as Burtweed had shut the door on the clergy. 'What the devil do I know about these things?' he said. 'Has the whole ship's company gone mad?'

'Oh, it's only Red Sea nerves, sir,' was the unconcerned reply. 'We always expect an epidemic of complaints in the heat. Just give them the usual Company's guff.'

'The usual Company's guff!' Ebbs growled. As he picked up his knife and fork and poked at a cold sausage, a heavy woman with a snivelling daughter burst through the doorway and threw several closely-written sheets of ship's notepaper on his desk.

'One of your officers,' she said, 'sent my daughter that.'

Ebbs looked at the first lines:

'On watch below the tropic moon
I think of thee and thy sweet breast,
Ah, midnight comes! But not too soon,
I'll creep to where thou lie at rest...'

'Present my compliments to Mr Jay,' he told Burtweed without reading further. 'And ask him to come to my cabin after his watch.'

The mother was followed by Dancer, who accused his cabin steward of using make-up. Behind him was an honest English bricklayer, an emigrant from the eight-berth cabins on C deck, a sturdy voyager who refused to strike his bowler and braces in the climate.

'I don't want you to think I'm making trouble, sir,' he said, gazing respectfully at Ebbs' gold epaulettes. 'I ain't the sort. Live and let live, that's my motto. Always has been. If the missus and me is parked in different cabins for the trip – well, fair enough, we're having it on the cheap. And I'm a broadminded man myself, Captain, take it from me. When the blokes in my cabin woke up yesterday morning and saw that 'airdresser from Blackpool with a little redheaded bit in bed with him – why, we choked him off about it, and 'nuff said. But this morning me missus wakes up – and I ask you! There he is, sleeping like a babe with the same piece, among seven other ladies.'

'Burtweed,' Ebbs said when the bricklayer had been hastened away with a vague promise of stricter segregation. 'No one else is to be admitted to my cabin – no one. I am feeling extremely unwell, I have hardly started my breakfast, and I am in no mood to listen to the idiotic outpourings of passengers. Say that I'm steering the ship.'

'Very good, sir.'

'Yes, Sparks?' he asked, as the Senior Radio Officer came timidly to the door. He was a small diffident man with thick spectacles.

'Do you think this ought to go off, sir?' he inquired, handing Ebbs a cablegram. 'After what you said about passengers' messages at Suez, I thought I'd better bring it down.'

Ebbs read it:

MCWHIRREY BINNICLE LONDON
SUBVERSIVE RED BOLSHIE INFLUENCE RAMPANT
ABOARD DISGUSTED BROSTER.

Ebbs looked at the paper for some time without expression. His feelings had already been bludgeoned into insensibility. 'Present my compliments to Brigadier Broster,' he asked Burtweed, wearily pushing aside his knife and fork. 'And ask him to step up to my cabin.'

'It's an outrage!' Broster shouted as soon as he appeared.

'But perhaps, Brigadier, if you would reconsider this cable… '

'Why should I?'

'It might cause unnecessary alarm in the head office,' Ebbs said, as calmly as possible. 'Or in ships picking it up at sea. They might think it was mutiny.'

'I don't withdraw a word.'

'I have of course the right to prevent any cable leaving the ship,' said Ebbs mildly.

'Adding the suppression of free speech to your other constitutional iniquities, eh?'

Ebbs scratched himself, sighed, then said appealingly, 'If only you'd lay your complaint before me, sir! Instead of going over my head to the Chairman – '

'There it is, Captain! There it is! Right in front of your nose! Look at it! Smell it! That devilish propaganda sheet, written on the orders of Moscow from beginning to end, I shouldn't be surprised!'

Broster's finger pointed accusingly at the page of stencilled foolscap lying by Ebbs' cold breakfast. It was headed:

THE CHARLEMAGNE TIMES
SHIP'S NEWSPAPER
Good Morning, Everybody!

This, the *Charlemagne's* only acknowledgement of an outside world, was composed in the early morning in the wireless office from items generously poured out in morse from England. As the personal caprice of the operator was its only sub-editor, it achieved, like all ship's newspapers, flashes of contrast and curiosity that could have sat creditably on the pages of the *Daily Mirror.*

'Read that, Captain!' commanded Broster, glaring at the Radio Officer.

Ebbs started at the beginning.

Racing Results. Racing at Newcastle. 1.30: Lucky Lucy (6/4), Highway (100/6), Pow-wow (3/1). 2.00: Boyo (10/1), Grantchester (6/4), William the Conk (100/8). 2.30: Lord Hornblower (6/4), The Duke (5/1), Impasse (100/8).

Football. The English International centre forward Gorringe is receiving massage and heat treatment for the knee injury sustained in last week's cup-tie. It is expected that he will be fit enough to lead his club's attack in their needle match next Saturday against Arsenal. It is officially stated by his club that the inner ligament of his knee, which caused him to drop out of last month's International, is not causing trouble. There is a deep cut about an inch long below the right edge of the knee-cap. Gorringe netted four goals before he was injured last week, and has now notched sixteen goals in five matches. He is not under official training, but is said to be keeping fit by digging in his garden. Gorringe is a keen amateur gardener, and grows all his own vegetables.

London. The Cabinet resigned today.

Cricket, Sydney. The Sheffield Shield match between New South Wales and Victoria is causing unprecedented excitement as it nears its closing stages. Today will tell if the Victoria batsmen can make the remaining 214 runs on a turning wicket rapidly deteriorating in one of the most phenomenal summers in Sydney's history. A Sydney spokesman yesterday described the weather of the last week as 'The greatest disaster in the history of New South Wales'.

New York. The President of the United States was assassinated this afternoon.

Paris. The Government fled because of revolution which broke out here yesterday.

Billiards. Mr Harry Evershed, the billiards and snooker champion, has recovered from a mild bout of influenza and will be able to compete in the snooker championship next month at Thurston's as arranged. Harry Evershed, who has now won the championship six times, is also holder of the world's record for a break at blindfold snooker.

Goole. Addressing a Labour Party Rally here last night, Mr Harry Cropper said: 'The privileged and protected classes are again on the run, and they know it. They have been hiding behind the barricades of the rising cost of living, but honest working folk like you and me will stand no nonsense and intend to ferret them out. Ever since Labour first came to power in 1945, after those terrible years of Tory misrule that we remember, you and me, though others are beginning to forget, this country has gone forward with the people, not backward with the bankers.' (Cheers and laughter.) 'Let me tell you… '

His speech filled the rest of the page.

'Not very informative, possibly,' Ebbs said. 'But hardly traitorous.' He placed the paper on the toast-rack. 'We live a detached life at sea and tend to develop different values, I'm afraid.'

'Football, racing, cricket!' Brigadier Broster said savagely. 'And nothing else every morning except half a page of some Labour claptrap. You wouldn't think the Conservative Party existed. Propaganda, that's what it is!'

'Do you take the ship's press, Sparks?' Ebbs asked.

'Oh, no, sir! It's the young Second.'

'Is he a man of – ah, radical views?'

'Well, he talks a lot, sir.'

'What about this racing? What possible interest has that?'

'The crew, sir.'

'But damn it, they hardly see a horse from one year's end to another!'

'The Barman runs a book, sir. Captain Buckle tried to stop it, but he had trouble from the union.'

'You see?' Ebbs looked helplessly at Broster. 'Very good, Sparks. Please take press yourself in future. And let me see it before it's duplicated. Even if it means waking me every morning at six.'

'Now, about my cable – ' Broster began, as the Sparks left.

Ebbs held up a hand. He stood up, and began pacing his cabin.

'Brigadier Broster,' he said. 'I only ask for fairness. You know well enough the circumstances under which I hold this command. You know the difficulties that beset me on all sides. And the voyage is not yet half over. All I need is the chance to find my feet properly. I assure you that I am doing my best.'

'I have my duty to the Line's shareholders.'

'I only ask for a chance – that's all.'

'Captain, the Pole Star Line cannot afford to give chances – '

Ebbs interrupted him. 'Please see my point, sir. Supposing you had some fellow from the War Office forever looking over your shoulder when you were commanding your – your regiment. Surely, sir, you understand?'

Broster paused. He had held a temporary commission in the Pay Corps, but he never corrected the compliment of a more aggressive command.

'Well,' he said.

Ebbs gripped Broster's arm. 'And the help you could be to me, sir! You, whose experience of handling men – whose commercial genius – is foolishly allowed to run to waste on board.'

'I…'

'Yes, sir!' Ebbs pressed his advantage. 'If it were not that I hesitated to burden you, I should have already asked you to do even more for the ship. I know you run the deck-tennis competition, the shuffle-board tournament, the horse-racing, the daily sweep, the debating society, and bingo. If there is any other activity – '

Broster hesitated. He grunted. 'I'd thought of giving a talk on my experiences in China.'

'And so you shall, sir. And so you shall! This very night. There will be a large audience. I shall see to it myself. And any other function – ?'

Ebbs was startled to see Brigadier Broster blush.

'I've always wanted to read the lesson in Church.'

'Next Sunday! I shall inform the Canon.'

'I've already suggested it,' Broster admitted. 'But the damned fellow objected.'

'You leave it to me, sir! I'll fix him. Meanwhile, your cable… '

Broster hesitated. 'On this occasion,' he said, reluctantly crumpling the form, 'I shall overlook it. But this is your last chance, Captain.'

'I shall need no other.'

'I'll hold you to it, mind!' He wagged his finger in Ebbs' face. 'And to your other promises!'

'Of course, sir. I shall keep my word, never fear. Good day to you, sir.'

'Good day to *you*, Captain!'

When he had gone, Ebbs sat at his desk with his head in his hands.

'Tell any other callers,' he said hollowly, hearing Burtweed enter, 'that I have passed away.'

'Very good, sir.'

'And present my compliments to Canon Swingle. Say Brigadier Broster will be reading the lesson on Sunday. Both of them. Tell the Canon that if he refuses I shall put him back at his old table. With the five others.'

'What about the hymns, sir?'

'We shall have the same ones, Burtweed. I fear we have not yet exhausted the perils of the sea.'

15

At Aden peace and silence fell upon the ship, last broken at Tilbury.

As the yellow quarantine flag came down from the bridge the passengers began scrambling for the shore like children out of school on a summer's afternoon. A flock of launches jogged them across the oily harbour to the narrow town beneath the sharp shoulders of the cliffs, where Europeans simmer and yawn through their tours of duty. Waiting in the flimsy waterfront shops, the sleek Arabic merchants in bright ballooning robes stood before their stocks of Indian sandals, Egyptian handbags, Japanese lighters, German watches, and American cameras. The eager explorers, who know from every English travel book since *Eothen* the importance of haggling in hot climates, scrambled ashore to strike hard bargains; but the shopkeepers simply bowed to each other with dignity and stroked their thick black whiskers, certain of easing their visitors from their money by nightfall as effortlessly and pleasantly as they digested their meals.

On board, Ebbs lay on his pink sofa trying to distract himself with Willy Boast's book *Batting an Eyelid*.

'How mightily the yeomen of England stood shoulder-to-shoulder throughout that arid day of battle!' he read. 'Rising Phoenix-like from the ashes of their first innings "to scorn delights, and live laborious days", they smote the Antipodean invaders hip and thigh, and all the ranks of Tuscany at the Nursery end could scarce forbear to cheer. The last English batsmen

"Two dogs of black Saint Hubert's breed,
Unmatched for courage, breath, and speed"

101

recalled for a glorious moment the shining days of the great Victor Trumper, or the golden era when the incomparable W G scattered runs from his willow cornucopia, or even when England's charm was "Get 'em in singles!" But alas! A fatal snick put the ball to "that two-handed engine" at the wicket. *Sed fugit interea, fugit irreparabile tempus!*'

Mystified, Ebbs turned to its companion volume from the ship's library, *The Gasworks End.* Opening it at random, he continued reading:

'There was magic in the Oval air that momentous evening! It touched the flashing blades of the English batsmen, it frisked Ariel-like round the crouching fielders, the very gasometers seemed ready to dance at Oberon's behest. The English Captain – "a verray parfit gentil knight" – recalled the great days of the shining Victor Trumper, or the bounteous times when the incomparable WG sowed runs from his willow seed-box, or even when England's watchword was "Get 'em in singles!" And in the evening tea and victory came together. *Fortis fortuna adiuvat!*'

Ebbs threw the books on the deck and stood up. He scratched himself vigorously. His spots had coalesced overnight into large pink puffy patches, which gave him the feeling of having just donned a new woolly vest inside out.

He picked up his cap and stepped on to the brilliant deck, with the demeanour of a man following his last childhood to the graveyard. The ship was empty. The decks rang only to the leisurely footsteps of unbidden stewards, the ebullient table-tennis balls were stilled, deck quoits lay forlornly in the scuppers, and the saloons were bare except for Willy Boast snoring in his usual corner of the smoke-room. Ebbs savoured the sadly transient peace. Below him, the last half-filled launch burst noisily from the ship's side, and he saw Mrs Porteous sitting in the stern close to a man in smart tropical clothes whom he recognised after an instant as Shawe-Wilson.

'Umm,' he said. He hoped they would keep each other occupied.

The Chief Engineer, his face fiery and thickly spattered with sweat, came slowly puffing up the ladder in an oily boiler-suit.

'How much longer at bunkers, Mr Earnshawe?'

Earnshawe wiped his face with a scrap of cotton waste. 'We're only just started. Another ten hours, I'd say.'

Ebbs glanced at his watch. 'Away by midnight then?' Earnshawe nodded. Together they leaned on the hot varnished teak of the rail, gazing at the shimmering inhospitable coast beyond the lines of refuelling ships.

'Not an attractive spot,' Ebbs said.

'No,' Earnshawe agreed, after considering the remark for some time. 'Still, it gives the passengers a run ashore.'

'Passengers!'

For a minute or so the two men stayed silent. Then on an impulse, Ebbs asked, 'Have a drink, Chief?'

Earnshawe thought over the suggestion carefully. 'Aye, I don't mind if I do.'

In his cabin Ebbs rang the bell repeatedly. But Burtweed was far beyond call, soaking his feet. 'Lord knows what happens to the Tiger in port,' he grumbled. He scratched himself and rummaged in the cocktail cabinet for a whisky bottle and two glasses. 'It is somewhat remiss of me not to have asked you up before, Chief,' he added apologetically, setting the drinks between them. 'I suppose in the old *Luther* McNair and I looked at each other's faces over every meal for the best part of five years. But in this ship you don't seem to get time to see anyone you want to.'

'Don't give it a second thought, Captain,' Earnshawe said gruffly. 'I know what you're up against. Yours is a full-time job, and no mistake. This for me?' He picked up a glass half full of neat whisky and swallowed it.

'I wish I could say that others appreciated my position half as much,' Ebbs continued, moodily sipping his drink. 'I don't want to tell tales out of school, Chief – but damn it! The way my Chief Officer treats me is a scandal.'

'I never did care much for that Shawe-Wilson. A good kick up the bottom wouldn't do him any harm.'

'And some of the passengers aren't much better. Brigadier Broster, for instance... I'm not a malicious man, Chief, but by God! I'd greatly like to tear his entrails out with my bare hands.'

'You want to put your foot down,' Earnshawe said chidingly, slapping the table with his hand. 'You're the Captain, aren't you?'

'Yes, I'm the Captain,' Ebbs admitted sadly. 'But my position in that capacity is somewhat…somewhat… ' He decided to say no more. 'Shall we have another drink?' he asked, as if suggesting a long walk on a wet day.

'I wouldn't say no.'

As Ebbs refilled the glasses Earnshawe leaned back, looked at him carefully, and declared, 'You have a hell of a life, lad, don't you?'

'Do you know, that's about the first kind word anyone's said to me since we left Tilbury,' Ebbs told him gratefully. 'I know the Captain leads a somewhat solitary existence – I'm used to that, sure enough, it was just the same for Nelson. But *this* ship! Do you know what I've had to put up with since Suez?' He felt the stimulation of a sympathetic ear, and continued, 'Complaints, complaints, complaints! "Captain, someone's writing poetry to my daughter… Captain, someone's chucked their breakfast down my waistcoat… Captain, my bedroom steward wears powder and scent…" Why, they hold me responsible for everything on board from their burnt tea-cakes to the political colour of the ship's newspaper. It's damnably unfair!'

'We always get it in the Red Sea,' Earnshawe said calmly. 'It's the heat, and being on top of each other from morning to night with sweet fanny to do. The passengers aren't used to it like we are. If they didn't let off steam by crabbing there'd be bloody murder in the passenger decks.'

'Not an unattractive alternative,' Ebbs said solemnly. He finished his drink in a gulp, and coughed mildly.

'I'm not a drinker,' Ebbs explained, pouring out more whisky. 'In fact, I can go from one voyage to the next without a drop. But I must admit, Chief, there are occasions when a glass of spirits doesn't come amiss.'

'Aye,' Earnshawe agreed. 'You've got to keep the machinery oiled.'

'How about you, Chief? How do you get on with the passengers?'

'Oh, I try and make a go of it.' Earnshawe picked up a pencil lying on the table and ruminatively began picking his teeth. 'I'm a good engineer – I know that. Might as well be honest about it. I reckon I deserve a good ship under me. And so I play the Social Joe to order. I've no alternative if I don't want to sweat my guts out in some third-rate tramp, I've got to pin on a dickey and act the bloody gigolo. It's part of the job. I don't like carrying passengers, that's straight. I don't like carrying cattle, and they're a bloody sight more untidy in their habits.'

'It's different for me,' Ebbs said, feeling the stirrings of self-pity. 'I've always wanted to command a passenger ship. Always. Ever since I was a cadet so high. It's been the only ambition in my life.'

'My ambition,' Earnshawe said, 'is to run a farm.'

'A farm?'

'Yes. Slap in the middle of the country. Where you can't even smell the sea in a high wind and the only sailors you have to look at are on cigarette packets. I want to walk round my own land, with a gun under my arm and a dog at my heels.' He put down the pencil, and began moving his empty glass round the table-top in thoughtful circles. 'That's all I want from life. Nothing more. I've got my eye on a place, too.' He stared for a while through the porthole at the hazy Aden cliffs. 'It's about the right size. A good bit of land. On the edge of the Wolds, five miles the York side of Market Weighton. I know the fellow who farms it. I can have it any time I like, more or less.'

'When are you going to buy it?'

'Oh...one day. When the wife's pools come up.'

They sat in sad silence for some time. Ebbs refilled the glasses.

'You married, Captain?'

'No. Yes,' Ebbs said. He reached for Burtweed's picture from the pipe-rack. 'The wife and kids,' he explained.

Earnshawe studied the photograph steadily for a minute. 'They're like you,' he decided.

Ebbs nodded, and replaced it.

'It's a grand institution, the family,' Earnshawe said. 'A grand institution. You can't get away from it – there's place like home, as long as it's your own.'

'Quite,' Ebbs said.

'To our wives, God bless 'em!' Earnshawe raised his glass.

'To our wives.'

'Drink up, Captain,' Earnshawe said, smacking his lips 'Let's have another.'

Some time later, Ebbs became more cheerful. 'Wouldn't it be fun, Chief,' he said with a giggle, 'to sail now and leave the ruddy passengers on the beach?'

The Chief Engineer considered the proposition for a while, rubbing his face forcefully with his palm. 'No,' said. He shook his head. 'It wouldn't be right, that wouldn't.'

'Perhaps not. Still, it's an idea.' Ebbs stuck his hand inside his shirt and scratched his chest. 'This itch is enough to make a saint swear,' he grumbled. Suddenly changing his mind, he kicked off his shoes under the table. 'And those bloody buckskins draw my feet something cruel in hot weather. I don't like 'em, but I've got to wear 'em. Why? Because I'm the ruddy Captain, that's why. In the old *Luther* now, I used to have plimsolls. I could wear what liked in the *Luther.* Nothing at all if I fancied. She wasn't a bad old ship in many ways,' he reflected, as if recalling an unhappy childhood.

'You'll not see the inside of that tub again.'

'I'm not so sure, Chief, I'm not so sure,' he said. He glanced through the open cabin door down the long, clean, empty, sun-drenched deck, and after a pause whispered, 'Quiet, Chief, isn't it?'

Half an hour later Earnshawe picked up the whisky bottle from the deck.

'Why, it's empty!' Ebbs said in surprise. 'But there's lots more in the cocktail thing. Pour out another drink and I'll tell you my secret. Do you want to know what it is?'

Earnshawe shook his head. 'I don't like hearing secrets. Then I don't have to keep 'em.'

Ebbs giggled. 'I'll tell you. I've had a woman in my cabin.'

'Oh, women!' Earnshawe dismissed the commonplace.

'She didn't stay, though.' Ebbs smiled wistfully. 'I quite wish she had now. Where are you going?' he added suspiciously, as Earnshawe got up.

'Down below. We're still bunkering.'

'Oh, are we?'

'I'd turn in lad, if I was you.'

'I'm not drunk, you know,' Ebbs replied in carefully-reasoned tones. 'I haven't been drunk since…since, oh, since last Christmas Good Friday.'

'I'd turn in, all the same.'

'S'long, Chiefy old lad. You're a damn good scout. Damn good. A damn good scout.'

They shook hands ardently, and for a minute or so stood slapping each other on the back.

'Goodbye, Chiefy, old man!'

'Goodbye, Captain!'

When Ebbs was alone he fetched a new bottle from the cocktail cabinet and poured himself another drink. As he noticed the whisky splash over the table vague feelings of guilt lumbered through his mind, but they disappeared immediately again into the fog. Life seemed suddenly all contentment. He began to sing.

On the boat-deck immediately below his open cabin door Mrs Judd looked up in annoyance. She had shared Ebbs' appreciation of the empty and silent decks, for she was a kind-hearted woman who had automatically achieved the position on board of the ship's Good Sport. If anyone wanted a dress mended, a baby watched, a confession consoled, or a romance manoeuvred, they unhesitatingly came to Mrs Judd. Now she had settled in the outrageous luxury of a deck-chair occupied since Gibraltar by the fierce-eyed wife of a General, enjoying for a few hours the impossibility of having to make up a fourth at bridge, read fairy tales to children, accompany a contralto against the distant glory of the ship's concert, or interpret for some idiotic girl the obvious intentions of her gallant. And some oaf of a sailor had ruined it by singing rowdily on the bridge.

The tune ceased. Ebbs appeared in his doorway.

'Good afternoon, Captain,' she said. She smiled. She liked Ebbs, whose unkempt appearance and desperately persevering good manners awoke maternal instincts in any good woman.

'Madam,' he said. He saluted with a flourish.

He gripped the rail, came carefully down the ladder, and saluted again. 'Your servant,' he said. 'May I sit?'

'Of course, Captain!'

He took the chair next to her.

'The ship's very quiet, isn't it?' she said.

'We're alone,' Ebbs told her solemnly.

'Why, Captain!' She began to laugh. 'You haven't got any shoes on!'

Ebbs glanced with surprise at his feet.

107

'Nor have I!' he exclaimed. He turned and looked at her steadfastly. 'I have the devil of a life,' he said. 'The devil of a life. Nobody loves me. Nobody cares about poor old Ebbs. Nobody minds if I were dead and bloody well buried.' Two tears ran towards his sharp cheekbones and dropped heavily over the edge.

'Captain, really!' she said. She laughed again. 'I do believe you've been drinking.'

'I'm a drunken beast,' Ebbs said, with some pride.

'Well, I'm sure you're entitled to be.'

'You understand, don't you?' Ebbs asked earnestly. 'You'll give me a kind word? Let me hold your hand. Where is it? Ah, thank you, madam. Thank you. I need kindness. Nobody's kind to me any more.' He gazed at her tragically, and shook his head. 'You're devilishly attractive,' he said.

'Hadn't you better be going back to your cabin?'

'Why?'

'The deck steward will be along in a minute with my tea.'

'What's that got to do with it?'

'I think perhaps you'd better.' She stood up. 'Come along, now.'

'But I want to stay here!' Ebbs insisted.

'Come along,' she said firmly. She took his arm. 'That's right, Captain. I'll help you up the ladder.'

In his cabin, Ebbs grabbed Burtweed's photograph and said: 'Little woman and little ones. See?'

'Very charming. Now, where's your bunk?'

Ebbs took on an outraged expression. 'No you don't!' he cried. 'No, you don't! I know your type!' He shook a finger at her, overbalanced, and grabbed her shoulders for support. 'You – you – ' He began to giggle. 'You wouldn't be the first one,' he said coyly.

'I'm sure I wouldn't. Ah, through there I see. Now come along, Captain. That's the way. All right, hold my hand if you want to. Mind the step – careful!'

She thoughtfully turned on the fan and drew the curtains before leaving. When Burtweed came up at six Ebbs was lying on his back in his uniform, his mouth open and clutching in both arms the end of his voice-pipe. He looked like a child with his favourite teddy-bear.

16

Ebbs was gazing with silent reproof into the mirror that he was using to rehearse his penitence the next morning when Burtweed entered his cabin. The *Charlemagne* was at sea again. At midnight Ebbs had taken her out of harbour, dosing himself with coffee and aspirin, and in a corrosive temper. He had dozed until dawn, fretted through the humid early morning, and summoned Mrs Judd as soon as he dared after breakfast.

'What the devil could have happened to me, Burtweed?' he demanded. 'Did I go mad? Was I possessed?' He suddenly struck the top of his dressing-table. 'Damnation! The care I've taken to preserve my good name on board! Then I go and get drunk in port like some first-trip fourth mate. Worse than that. I molest women.'

'One thing leads to another, so they say, sir,' Burtweed said gravely.

Ebbs groaned. Black disgrace and despair lay upon him. The female now stamping indignantly towards his cabin had probably already sealed a scandalised note to McWhirrey, explaining that the Captain of the *Charlemagne* got sozzled in port and outraged the female passengers. After that, even the *Martin Luther* would be too good for him.

'But why, why on earth, did I do it?'

'I've seen it happen very sudden with Captains during the war, sir. Release from strain they called it.'

'Possibly. But I am no longer braving torpedoes, Burtweed, merely the opinion of my passengers.'

'The madam, sir,' Burtweed announced, withdrawing briskly.

'My dear good lady – ' Ebbs began ardently, bounding across his day-cabin. 'How can I possibly tell you – have a chair, please – how can I possibly explain my conduct? How can I assure you that yesterday I was not myself? How can I apologise? Madam, I entreat you to believe – '

'Please, Captain!' she held up a hand, and smiled at him sympathetically. 'Don't worry about yesterday another little bit.'

'Surely you must think me a degenerate of the lowest type?'

'Not in the slightest,' she said cheerfully. 'You were perfectly charming. May I have a cigarette?'

'Yes, of course… ' Ebbs jumped forward with his sociable cigarettes, spilling most of them on the deck. 'I recall – with the deepest shame, madam, but I recall it – thrusting my attentions on you on the boat-deck.'

'Now don't say another word,' she told him firmly, smiling again. 'I only gave you a helping hand. Just as – well, your wife would have done.'

'My wife? Yes, of course.' Ebbs abruptly sank into a chair.

'You mean,' he continued anxiously, hope beginning to shine on him faintly, 'you don't intend to complain about my behaviour? I assure you, with all fairness, madam, you are more than entitled to. I have no desire to shirk the just – '

'You're completely forgiven,' she said with finality. 'Let's just forget the whole thing.'

'Mrs Judd,' Ebbs blew his nose 'You are very, very good.'

'Not a bit. I'm sure you more than deserved your party. May I have a match?'

'Yes, yes, certainly… '

'Thank you, Captain. And don't worry – I shan't say a word to anyone.'

'You are indeed a paragon of virtue,' Ebbs said with deep relief. He wondered for an instant about the effect on the ship of two rumours circulating from different women that he was an impotent prude and a drunken lecher. 'Though I can hardly believe I deserve your goodness. You see, there are certain circumstances connected with the command of this ship,' he confessed, 'which make my position somewhat difficult. A complaint of any sort might have a most unfortunate effect. I am really trying to do my best – '

'Of course you are, Captain! Why, the way you handle those terrible people at the table is nothing short of magnificent.'

'Do you really think so?' he asked eagerly.

'Aren't they an awful bunch?'

'Well, madam, it is hardly my position…'

'That man Broster! Isn't he the biggest bore in Christendom? Why, the number of times I've wanted to throw the cruet at him!'

Ebbs nodded warmly. 'How you echo my own sentiments, dear madam!'

'And isn't that child Annette infuriating? If only she'd learn another two words her conversation might be almost tolerable. And as for Mr Dancer –'

'An effeminate type, I think?'

'Oh, very. And Mrs Porteous –'

'Ah, Mrs Porteous!'

'Boast is merely disgusting –'

'Quite. And the Cokes –'

'I do wish they'd keep their room. Now Mrs Lomax –'

'Surely she's a harmless old lady?'

'Harmless? Good gracious, no! She gossips like poison.'

'Does she indeed? A reprehensible habit. Particularly in ships.'

'Oh, very.'

Ebbs blew his nose again. He felt the same unbelievable happiness that had overwhelmed him in McWhirrey's office.

'Just look at your hands!' Mrs Judd exclaimed. 'Why, you poor man – you're absolutely covered with urticaria.'

'It was the fish,' Ebbs murmured, as if apologising for it.

'But you must be in torment! No wonder it drove you to drink.'

'The irritation is certainly an added trial.'

'I've got something in my cabin that'll fix it in a jiffy. I'll send my steward up with it. And your cuff, Captain!' She laughed as she caught sight of a tear on the sleeve of Ebbs' white jacket, which he had mended with the Company's paper-stapler.

'The Captain certainly mustn't go about dressed like that. If you'll let me have it this evening I'll stitch it for you. Well,' she said, rising, 'I'm sure you've lots of important things to do, Captain. And I've to play my deck-tennis heat. It's with Brigadier Broster, and he becomes rather upset if anyone is late. So we'll meet at lunch.'

'Yes, of course.' Ebbs looked at her with admiration. 'Perhaps you would honour me by taking a liqueur after dinner this evening?'

'I'd be absolutely charmed. In the smoke-room?'

'It is customary for the Captain to entertain in his cabin… '

'I'd be even more honoured. After dinner, then? Good morning, Captain.'

'Good morning to you, dear lady… ' Ebbs blew his nose loudly again, and when he looked up Mrs Judd had gone.

17

'Heart of oak are our ships!' sang Brigadier Broster lustily, as though demanding his lunch. 'Heart of oak are our men! We always…are ready! Steady, boys, steady! We'll fight and we'll conquer again…and again! A-gain and again! A-gain and…again!'

He bowed. The audience expressed its relief in applause.

It was a week later. The weather was cooler, the companionable flying fish danced less thickly round the *Charlemagne's* bows, and her social progress neared its climax with the ship's concert. Brigadier Broster had insisted on setting up as impresario, and arranged the bill like the second house at the Palladium with himself the star turn. After half a dozen of the passengers had briefly trod the boards rigged by the Bos'n on the boat-deck, Broster strode firmly before the backcloth of mixed ensigns to finish the performance alone. He had already done three-card tricks, recited *Boots,* told several stories about Irishmen and Scotsmen, turned a hard-boiled egg into a billiard ball, imitated birds, and sung What *Shall We Do with the Drunken Sailor?* and according to the programme he had still to render *A Wandering Minstrel I* and *Rule Britannia* before capitulating to the National Anthem.

Mrs Judd, sitting in the front row of deck-chairs with Ebbs, touched him on the hand and whispered: 'Do you think we can escape?'

Ebbs nodded. They guiltily slipped from their places while Broster was noisily arranging his larynx for the next song.

'I'd much rather be talking to you, William,' she said, smiling up at him as they walked gently forward along the deserted deck. 'So much rather.'

'Dear Edith,' Ebbs said solemnly. 'How very sincerely I feel the same.' He blew his nose loudly.

For the past few days Ebbs had been weathering an invigorating emotional storm. A ship in hot weather is a fine incubator for intimacies, and within an hour of first settling herself with a Green Chartreuse in his cabin Mrs Judd had revealed that her name was Edith, that she was a widow, her husband had grown tobacco in Rhodesia, she was going to stay with a sister in Sydney whom she hadn't seen for fifteen years, she was fond of Sealyhams and long walks, couldn't stand bananas, preferred the cold but was subject to chilblains, and thought T S Eliot was terrific. At the same time she discovered that Ebbs was passionately fond of sherry trifle, was frightened of bats, had a brother who came to a bad end in Canada, and wanted to find a way of making white collars last longer at sea.

The next day Ebbs was amazed how coincidence repeatedly thrust them together. Whenever he appeared on deck he either stumbled across her steamer chair or happened to find her taking the air on the rail outside his cabin. By the following night he had learned that she married her husband a week after meeting him, was thirty-two last birthday, slept in bed-socks in winter, had an operation for appendicitis when she was twelve, thought Ebbs was the most loveable man she had ever seen, and wore her stockings rolled below her knees in hot weather. She simultaneously found that Ebbs had an ingrowing toenail, was once almost engaged to a New Zealand girl who abandoned him for an Auckland pork-butcher, felt depressed in the tropics, thought she was the most sympathetic woman in the world, used to play the flute, and hated onions.

'How awful that we'll soon have to part!' she sighed. They were leaning on the rail where Priscilla had thrown the red lead at Ebbs. From aft came faint sounds of the latest assault on Gilbert and Sullivan.

'But I trust not for ever, my dear,' Ebbs said wistfully. 'After all, the end of the voyage is by no means the end of the world.'

She gazed for a while at the faint change in shade that represented the horizon.

'Dear William!' She took his hand. 'But what about your wife and family?'

'Ah, my wife and family.'

'You always become so – so sad when you speak of them.'

'Do I?'

'Yes, always. Is there – forgive me, William, I suppose it's really very naughty and none of my business – but is there any…difficulty?'

Ebbs shrugged his shoulders. 'Only – up to a point, you might say.'

'She looks very charming from her photograph.'

'You think so?'

'Yes. And your children. I suppose it must be wonderful, your welcome home when you've been so long at sea?'

'Oh, wonderful.'

'Do the children take after you or after her?'

'Have you noticed the phosphorescence on the water? Remarkably consistent in these latitudes.'

She sighed again. 'I suppose really it must be heartbreaking being married to a sailor. Your wife must seem quite a stranger to you sometimes.'

'Quite a stranger.'

'And then, while you're away…men like you, who are so attractive to women… '

'Oh, tut!' Ebbs protested.

'But it's true. I really mean it. You could have the heart of any woman on board – and you've picked on me,' she said with flattering satisfaction.

'You don't suppose anyone's noticed it?' Ebbs asked, suddenly pricked with anxiety.

'Oh, no! Not at all.'

'I should hate to be talked about. And my position – '

'Tell me all about your home,' she said softly. 'And your troubles.'

For a second the tropical breeze that gently rustled her dress tempted Ebbs to tell her the truth about Burtweed's photograph. But the sailor's caution which lurked in his subconscious, that safeguarded ships manoeuvring in unknown currents and fog, made him say instead, 'It's really a subject of very little interest.' Applause from the other end of the deck indicated that Broster had finished. 'Perhaps we should be returning? I gather it's my duty to buy all the performers a drink.'

'But can't we have a nightcap afterwards?'

He patted her hand. 'Of course, Edith.'

'That will be lovely! Then I can finish darning your socks.'

Ebbs was a simple man, who had never had an affair since his disillusionment over the Auckland butcher, and he believed that his romance would go unnoticed by his passengers. But they had as little chance of ignoring it as a green-spotted sea serpent surfacing off the port bow. He pranced round the deck distributing smiles as lavishly as the sea water from the Bos'n's morning hose-pipe, and now forced the table talk in the saloon like a hearty housemaster at the first supper of term. He patted children on the head, helped old ladies from their deck-chairs, and even cheeked Brigadier Broster, while every morning the ship's gossips raked his character thoroughly with their sharp tongues. To the officers, Mrs Judd had come as the thawing sun of springtime. A captain of good moods is sufficient to turn the most uncomfortable tramp into a happy home, but a captain in love affects the ship's company like a rise in pay. Ebbs began slapping the Mates jovially on the back, forgot about the chartroom pencils, told Jay not to overtax his strength, and even made jokes on the bridge. Before long the *Charlemagne* had become one of the happiest ships afloat.

But one member of the crew disapproved.

'A charming woman, Mrs Judd,' Ebbs declared cheerfully to Burtweed over breakfast, the morning after the concert.

'Yes, sir.' He morosely collected Ebbs' dirty linen into its daily bundle.

'Such a sensible down-to-earth person,' he continued, taking up half a kidney. 'So frank and open. Not like some others I could name on board.'

'No, sir.'

'And she is a remarkable help to me in the ship. Over all sorts of problems.' He enumerated them with his knife. 'How to give the prizes for the children's sports, for instance. What to say to this impossible woman whose daughter's caught up with some tourist-class Romeo. How to pacify those females who tell me the ship's water ruins their hair or their underclothing. Furthermore, she completely cured my beastly spots. Oh, invaluable, invaluable!' he went on, readdressing himself to his breakfast. 'I only regret I had not made her acquaintance more fully earlier in the voyage.'

'Yes, sir.'

Ebbs looked up sharply. 'Burtweed,' he said, 'do I take it from your manner that you disapprove of my remarks?'

'Yes, sir.'

Ebbs slowly bisected a sausage. 'And why, pray?'

'Oh, sir!' Burtweed dropped the laundry, and stood before him with fingers entwined. 'Oh, sir! I shouldn't like to see you get caught, sir.'

'What on earth do you mean, man?'

'Oh, sir – forgive me, sir! I speak from the fullness of heart – but there's many a captain I've seen carried away, as it were, sir, right on his first voyage, before he's got wise to the tricks, sir.'

'Burtweed, you are talking nonsense. The lady is the soul of honour. And anyway, merely a companion.'

'I'd not say a word against the madam, sir. Not a word. But now she does your socks and your clothes, sir, and tidies up your cabin... '

'The feminine touch, Burtweed.'

'But that's my job, sir. You're *my* Captain, sir – not the madam's.'

'God bless my soul, Burtweed, you're jealous!'

'Besides, sir – is it *right?*'

'Right? My good man,' Ebbs told him sternly, 'there is not the slightest breath of impropriety... '

'But for a married man, sir!'

'But I'm not a married man, damn it!'

'Yes, sir. But you *tell* her you are, sir. Which is the same thing, sir.'

'Burtweed, you're impossible.'

'I have my standards, sir,' Burtweed said with dignity.

'Kindly keep them to yourself. Ah, Mr Shawe-Wilson,' Ebbs exclaimed as the Chief Officer appeared at the door. 'And a very good morning to you. Capital day, is it not? You're looking remarkably fresh. Taking a swim before breakfast, I hope? Excellent, excellent! Now, what can I do to assist you today?'

18

Later that morning Prittlewell stuck his head from the door of his office in the Square, and pointed at one of the bellboys who passed their days pinching each other's behinds on the bench outside. 'You, boy! Go and fetch me the Barman. And tell him to make it snappy.'

He polished his monocle, then gazed at the crowd of passengers jostling round the ship's bulletin boards. They all carried bundles of coloured material, rolls of *crêpe* paper, and bunches of funny hats, for the day of the ship's gala fancy dress dance had arrived. That night there would be jollity and balloons, souvenirs and prizes, the last swill of duty-free gin, the last burst of shipboard comradeship, the last kisses of moon-ridden romances: the voyage was now almost over, and roped trunks already stood in the alleyways among the cabin litter of dance programmes, menus, lottery tickets, race cards, and redeemed wine chits, thrown out like a schoolboy's treasures devalued by the holidays. The next day would be dedicated to hurried packing and would end quietly with the official sadness of the *dîner d'adieu,* then many of the passengers would be tipped on to the uncaring shores of Fremantle and leave the rest to haunt a joyless ship until Melbourne and Sydney.

'You've taken your time, haven't you?' Prittlewell snapped, when Scottie appeared. 'I haven't got all day to waste.'

'Very sorry, sir,' Scottie said humbly.

'I should think so. One of the passengers – Brigadier Broster, in fact – has complained you were insolent to him. What have you got to say to that?'

'I'm very, very sorry, sir.'

Several of the passengers looked sympathetically as the barman roasted in the blaze of Prittlewell's stare.

'Not only were you insolent, but he's reported that you made a mistake mixing his White Lady.'

'It won't happen again, sir.'

'It had better not,' Prittlewell continued loudly. 'Furthermore, he tells me that he suspects you have on occasion given him short measure.'

'Never, sir! Never!' Scottie was horrified. 'I'm an honest man, sir – everyone knows that in the Line. I'd rather die first, than give short measure, sir.'

'Come inside,' Prittlewell ordered. 'We must discuss this further.'

Scottie went into the office, put his feet on the desk, unhooked the high white collar of his jacket, pulled an old pipe from his trouser pocket, and began filling it from Prittlewell's tobacco jar.

'Well, Herbie boy,' he said as Prittlewell closed the door and locked it. 'We don't seem to have had much time for a chat this voyage.'

'You know what it is, Jim,' Prittlewell apologised. 'His Nibs up top.' He jerked a thumb towards the bridge. 'Best to keep up the old act good and strong.'

'Oh, you're right there, Herbie. Every time.' Scottie lit his pipe. 'Hear from the wife at Aden?'

'I had a line. She said your missus drove across with a nice side of bacon. Thanks a lot, Jim.'

'Think nothing of it, Herbie. After all, we're here on earth to help each other, aren't we? How's business at the hotel?'

'Can't complain, Jim. How's the farm?'

'Fair enough.'

'Let's have a drop of Scotch,' Prittlewell said, going to the locker. He winked. 'Not the stuff we give the customers, eh?'

When both were comfortable with their drinks, Scottie asked, 'How are we doing on the trip?'

Prittlewell unlocked a drawer in his desk and took out a small red cash-book. 'Here's the takings handed over to the Company to tally with stock,' he explained, indicating the figures with his fingers. 'And here's the cash you've taken at the bar. That leaves us – oh, about a thousand quid apiece.'

Scottie nodded thoughtfully. 'Could be better, I suppose. I promised the wife a new fur this voyage.'

Prittlewell agreed.

'It's difficult for a bloke to make a living these days,' Scottie observed. 'I've loaded the bottom of the measures as much as I dare. I stick in so much ice you can hardly get the drink in the glass. I had all that trouble with the Vichy water – '

Prittlewell grinned. 'You slipped up there Jim.'

'Well, how did I know they could see me at the tap? I ought to have put more Epsom salts in, I suppose. I'm getting old, Herbie, that's what it is. Losing the old touch.' He shook his head sadly. 'Sometimes I reckon it's almost time for me to retire ashore, and pay income tax like everyone else.'

'Go on with you, Jim. You're still one of the smartest in the game.' Prittlewell patted him affectionately on the shoulder. 'I tell you what. Tonight, I'll get 'em drinking champagne.'

'Ah, that would be something!' Scottie reflectively pushed down the tobacco in his pipe. 'I haven't had a good bash at the old champagne game for years now.'

'Leave it to me, Jim,' said Prittlewell, tapping his nose.

'How about the Old Man?' Scottie asked, pointing heavenwards.

'Leave him to me too,' Prittlewell said confidently.

The object of their anxiety was meanwhile standing in his vest in the middle of his cabin declaring to Burtweed: 'Come now! Let us dance!'

Burtweed hesitated.

'Hurry up, man! This is a matter to be taken with extreme seriousness.'

'Oh, sir!' Burtweed stuffed his duster into a trouser pocket and reluctantly stepped into Ebbs' embrace.

'You are the lady, Burtweed.'

'Yes, sir.'

'Right. We shall start. One moment – ' Ebbs glanced at a book in his hand, and from a page thickly trodden with ghostly footsteps read loudly: '"The gentleman starts with the left foot, inclining the weight of the body

slightly forward and progressing evenly with the sole of the whole foot."
Do you follow that, Burtweed?'

Ebbs, who was not a dancing man, usually avoided the nightly chalked
square on the *Charlemagne's* boat-deck. But Edith Judd had told him after
breakfast that she wanted the first waltz.

'Yes, sir.'

'We will begin when I give the signal. It's all perfectly simple. Ready?
One, two, three – go!'

Interlocked, they flailed across the cabin like a runaway threshing
machine.

'One – two – three, *one* – two – three, *one* – two – three!' Ebbs roared.
'Come along, man, come along!'

'Watch out, sir! Watch for the table, sir!'

'This is no time for timidity!' A table fell heavily to the deck, sending a
pink-and-gold standard lamp crashing into one of the clocks. 'One – two
– three, *one* – two – three – '

'Mind, Sir! My feet!'

'Then keep them out of the way, man! Put your back into it! One – two
– three, *one* – two – three – '

'The desk, sir! Look out – !'

'The other way, you fool! Keep it up, man, keep it up! One – two – '

Burtweed stopped and howled: Ebbs had crushed one of his toes.

'Perhaps rather more difficult than it appears,' Ebbs confessed cheerfully,
wiping his forehead. 'Where did you say you got this book from?'

'Off the cook, sir.' Burtweed looked reproachfully at him, caressing his
foot.

'Well, I must say he shows great aptitude. This is worse to follow than
The Channel Pilot. However, we shall persevere. Ready, Burtweed?'

'Oh, sir! Not again, sir?'

'Of course. That was the waltz, and now we shall learn the slow fox-
trot. You may be the gentleman this time. The hand goes in the small of
the back, so. Ah, good morning, Purser,' he said, pushing Burtweed
quickly aside. 'And what can I do for you?'

'I had come to discuss the arrangements for this evening, sir.' Prittlewell
was once again the smooth ocean aristocrat.

'Capital idea. You may go, Burtweed,' Ebbs added, as the Tiger limped away pointedly. 'Strange that the voyage should be almost over,' he continued sunnily to the Purser. 'A really excellent voyage it's been too! I must confess, I felt my difficulties at the beginning. But ever since Aden things seem to have got very much easier. Do you think, Purser – I am not seeking flattery or idle compliments, I assure you – but on the whole, would you say I was, well, a not unsuccessful Captain?'

'Most certainly, sir! And it has been a great pleasure to serve under your command.'

'Thank you, Purser, thank you.'

'I hope I shall continue to do so for many years, sir.'

'And I hope so, too.'

'Very kind of you, sir. In fact, I want to ask you to accept, as a personal token of my esteem, champagne for your table tonight at dinner.'

'Oh, come, come… '

'I'd far rather give it to you, sir, than allow it to stay untouched in the ship.'

'You mean, nobody on board drinks champagne?'

'Absolutely no one, sir. They seem to have lost the taste for it this voyage.'

'By Jove, Purser,' Ebbs said warmly. 'You leave it to me – I'll tell 'em all what jolly good champagne we've got on board, and they'll all be ordering it by the dozen at the dance.'

'That would be very good of you, sir.'

'Delighted, delighted.' The gong sounded below. 'What, lunch already? How time does fly. You'd better come back before dinner. I shall be turned in all afternoon.'

'I'm afraid not, sir. There's the children's tea-party.'

'Ah, the children's tea-party.' The single black cloud in Ebbs' sky crossed the sun. 'I suppose I really must go?'

'I don't think that Lady McWhirrey would like it otherwise, sir.'

'Very well. Perhaps one of the passengers – Mrs Judd, sitting at my table – might assist me. What time do I appear?'

'At three, sir. The children take a lot of interest in the Captain. They usually like to present him with a bunch of flowers or something of the sort.'

'Very charming, very charming. Well, I must get into lunch.'

'Perhaps you should put your shirt on first, sir?'

'Why, bless me, yes! Surprising how absent-minded I've become these days. Can't understand it.'

But Mrs Judd insisted that she was washing her hair that afternoon, and Ebbs had to reconcile himself to attending the tea-party alone.

19

By the time Ebbs approached the children's saloon he was filled with feeling of genuine benevolence. Usually he mistrusted infants, but his current emotional state clothed him spiritually in perpetual red gown and white whiskers. He decided he would pat a few convenient heads, distribute the small silver rattling specially in his pocket, accept the presentation bouquet with a few dignified words of one syllable then leave to continue his afternoon nap. He thought the experience would probably be both flattering and agreeable.

As he reached the saloon doors a spasm of discouragement ran through him. It sounded like a free fight in the fo'c'sle of the *Martin Luther.*

The Pole Star Line was proud of its catering for children, which was directed from London by Lady McWhirrey herself. They had their own chef, their own dining saloon decorated with bright bulbous animals, several nurseries filled with satisfyingly destructible toys, and a shaded pen on the boat-deck where they could be safely left while their parents went off and played. The herding and feeding of the *Charlemagne's* children was controlled by a motherly stewardess, assisted by half a dozen of the toughest and most trouble-making stewards on board, appointed by Prittlewell as an alternative to more unpleasant forms of punishment. From Tilbury to Fremantle the children wallowed in teas and similar entertainment, but they generously repaid the Line's attentions; alone of the passengers they still found every day a fresh excitement, and they nightly added to their prayers a whispered unofficial supplication that the voyage might never end.

When Ebbs opened the door the full force of the party struck him like a storm on deck. The saloon was filled with fairies, pirates, ballerinas, cowboys, pierrots, Pompadours, and pixies, all screaming and elbowing vigorously round long tables for the piles of food. The younger and more timid were pushed aside, squealing protests. If a small guest saw a smaller one with a tastier portion, he grabbed it. The older children near the door had struck a mutually advantageous truce, and ate steadily without acknowledging their neighbours; the youngest at the other end of the saloon looked upon eating only as an incidental to the main enjoyment of smearing the food on the bulkheads, the stewards, each other, and themselves; the children in the middle expressed the conflict of these two patterns of behaviour.

'God bless my soul!' exclaimed Ebbs.

'The Captain!' cried the motherly stewardess. She was a pink, grey-haired woman with a figure like a bunch of balloons. 'Look, kiddies!' She clapped her hands energetically. 'The Captain, kiddies! Come along now – take that jelly bowl off your head at once, Raymond, it's very naughty – here's the Captain! Say hello to the Captain! A big hello for the Captain, children – stop it immediately Mary, that's very rude – a big cheer, now – one, two, three… '

A roar of greeting came from every mouth, heavily muffled by masticating food.

Ebbs blew his nose. 'Ah – good afternoon, children,' he said, as though breaking serious news.

'I *am* glad you came, sir!' the stewardess told him happily. 'The dear little things think so much of the Captain. And aren't they having a wonderful time?' Her eyes were shining. 'Doesn't it do your heart good to see it, sir? Why, I don't think I'd miss the children's tea-party for the world. Now I'll take you round, sir, shall I?'

'Is it strictly necessary?' whispered Ebbs. As the children were now taking no notice of him and had noisily returned to assaulting their food and each other, he saw a chance of escape.

'But they'd be so disappointed if you didn't, sir.'

'Very well,' Ebbs said. 'I suppose it's my duty.'

'This is Terence,' she began brightly, starting with a pale child decorated with a florid pair of burnt-cork moustachios. 'Say hello to the Captain, Terence.'

Terence gave Ebbs a look of deep malevolence.

'Why, Terence!' she scolded. 'You haven't eaten up your nice ice-cream. You *are* a naughty boy!'

'Don't like it.'

'Come along now! Eat it up like a good little boy.'

'It's nasty.'

'Nonsense! Of course it isn't nasty. Not nasty at all, is it, Captain?'

'Not at all,' Ebbs murmured dutifully.

'Look,' she said, picking a large spoon from the table. 'The Captain will eat it. Won't you, Captain?'

She scooped melting pink ice-cream from the plate and offered it to Ebbs, who slowly opened his mouth and swallowed it.

'Jolly tasty,' he said grimly, trying to give the child a look of astonished appreciation. 'Yum, yum.'

'See, Terence? The Captain loves your nice ice-cream. This is Harriet,' she continued, switching him to a small and peaky fairy queen. 'What do you say to the Captain, Harriet?'

Harriet gave Ebbs a long look, and burst into tears. 'Goodness gracious!' Ebbs exclaimed. 'I trust I have not upset the poor child?'

'Oh, no, sir, she's always crying.' The stewardess flourished her experienced handkerchief. 'She's been crying almost continually since we left London. And what is it this time, Harriet?'

'Don't like my jelly,' Harriet sobbed.

'But it's beautiful jelly, Harriet! Isn't it, Captain?'

Ebbs nodded helpfully.

'Look, Harriet,' she picked up the child's own spoon. 'Watch the Captain – he loves your pretty jelly. Don't you, Captain?'

Ebbs took the orange jelly like castor oil.

'There now!' The stewardess returned the spoon triumphantly. 'I told you it was nice jelly. Eat it up now, or the Captain will finish the lot. And this is Robert,' she went on, reaching a small boy in sombrero and spurs, armed with a gun on each hip and one at the umbilicus. 'Why haven't you finished your sausage roll, Robert?'

'I think I must be getting back to the bridge – ' Ebbs began.

'Do stay just a little longer, sir! They love having you with them, the little dears.'

'Wanna banana!' screamed Robert.

The stewardess shook her finger. 'Now, now, Robert! You can't have a banana till you've finished your nice sausage roll.'

'Wanna banana!'

'Eat your lovely sausage roll like a good boy, or I'll be really cross. And so will the Captain.'

'Wanna banana!'

'But it's a scrumptious sausage roll. The Captain likes it, anyway. Don't you, Captain? Look, Robert – see how the Captain's enjoying your lovely sausage roll.'

'Wanna banana!' Robert insisted.

When Ebbs had stomached portions of blancmange, sardine sandwich, tangerine, chocolate icing, cheese spread, and nut cake, he said, 'Do you think we might try something else, Stewardess? I fear I am beginning to feel a little sick.'

'Of course, sir. We'll play games. They *do* love games, sir.' She clapped her hands. 'Come along, children! Hurry and finish up. The Captain wants to play.'

The children, who had now eaten themselves into nausea, streamed from the tables and surrounded Ebbs expectantly.

'What shall we play, children?' she asked. Immediately there was uproar. 'Musical chairs!'

'Postman's knock!'

'Ring-a-ring-o'-roses!'

'I spy!'

'Funny faces!'

'Murder!'

'Silence, children!' she called. 'Don't all speak at once. Wipe that trifle off your face, Ernest. We'll play blind man's buff. The Captain will be the blind man.'

'No, I won't!' Ebbs said.

'Very well, we'll play oranges and lemons. Hold hands, Captain. Here we go, children! Line up, now! Let that little boy go, Rosemary, you're hurting him. Ready, sir? One, two, three – *Oranges and Lemons, Said the Bells of St Clements...* '

The stewardess chanted gaily, they guillotined pairs of giggling children, and a deep sadness fell upon Ebbs. He recalled his seafaring career since he had first slung his hammock in the *Worcester* as an innocent overgrown lad. He saw himself stepping on to the deck of his first ship, an awkward cadet in a dangerously new uniform, off East for a two-year voyage in a rotting tramp with beetles for bed mates. Then working for his mate's ticket, struggling with books in his cabin and a merciless Captain on the bridge. Afterwards came his master's examination, following months ashore in chilly lodgings overshadowed with the fear of failure. Next the war, with every minute likely to conceal a torpedo. Unending freezing watches on a shaking bridge and warm bunks left bitterly at midnight; sweaty stops in breathless Eastern ports, fog in the Channel, and ice in the Atlantic; a pile of accumulated pains, which had raised him to his present job – playing oranges and lemons with the children.

His reflections were stopped by a child whisking off his cap.

'Give me that back!' Ebbs shouted.

'You naughty, naughty boy!' called the stewardess. 'Naughty little boy! Give the Captain his hat back, immediately!'

Ebbs' gold-peaked cap, decked with a stiff white tropical cover, went bouncing across the delighted children like a rubber ball on an ebbing tide.

'Give me that blasted cap!' he shouted, plunging after it.

'Give it back at once!' cried the stewardess, 'Jeanie... Charlie... Robin! At once, do you hear? The Captain doesn't want to play any more!'

By the time Ebbs had grabbed his cap, his white jacket and trousers looked like a nursery towel. He unthinkingly jammed it on his head, and felt something cold and sticky drop down his neck.

'I'm going to my cabin,' he announced with dignity.

The children roared with laughter, jumped up and down, and clapped their hands. What would the funny man do next?

'Oh, but sir!' cried the stewardess. 'Aren't you going to give away the presents?'

'I am certainly not going to give away any blasted presents to this pack of hooligans,' he said angrily. 'Good afternoon to you, stewardess. I trust you appreciate that you have ruined one complete set of whites? My laundry bill alone for this afternoon is considerable. The damage to my feelings is incalculable.'

'But please, sir,' she pleaded, 'wait for the presentation. Yes, I'm sure you will, sir! You can't go without the presentation. Where's the little girl who is going to give the Captain the bunch of flowers? Where are you, now? Little girl! Come along, little girl. Make haste! You mustn't keep the Captain waiting.'

A small girl with a large red paper rose in her hair, dressed in a grass skirt and a wholly anticipatory brassière, stepped forward with a handful of paper flowers. Ebb recognised his acquaintance Priscilla.

'So!' he exclaimed.

She stood silently before him, staring down meekly at her paper offering, as inoffensive as a cowslip.

'We have met before, young lady.' She said nothing.

'You are a very naughty girl,' Ebbs continued sternly.

'Whatever you did, say you're sorry to the Captain, dear,' the stewardess urged.

'I'm sorry,' she murmured.

'It was a shocking piece of behaviour,' Ebbs went on.

'I can't help it,' she said humbly. 'I'm maladjusted.'

'Well, you had better take pains to adjust yourself.' Feeling he had perhaps been too hard, Ebbs added more indulgently, 'Anyway, we can forget it now, can't we? As long as you're sorry there's no reason why we shouldn't be friends. But don't throw paint at people again. Now let us proceed with the ceremony. Are those lovely flowers for me?'

She looked up at him. 'Dear Captain – ' she began, in reproduction of a set speech. She paused. She opened and shut her mouth. Her usual poise was for once disturbed. 'Ooooo!' she said. Then she was sick all over his feet.

20

The *Charlemagne's* adult enjoyments began at nightfall. For a week the passengers had stitched and glued their costumes in the stuffy secrecy of their cabins; the barber's shop had been stripped of cosmetics, the Doctor's surgery raided for slings and eye-shades, trunks unwanted since Tilbury were mined from the baggage-room by sweating deckhands and every parson aboard forced to empty out his collar-box. At cocktail hour the passengers slipped shyly down the alleyways and burst into the smoke-room to gather applause for their ingenuity and needlework. Unfortunately, their inventiveness had run blindly down similar paths, and Scottie's cocktail shaker gathered squads of sailors and policemen, tribes of Bedouins and Zulus, convocations of clergy, a crèche of babies, and sufficient chefs to staff the Connaught Rooms.

'I congratulate you. I congratulate you all most warmly,' Ebbs said at dinner. He had recovered his composure and his appetite, and beamed round the heavily decorated table. 'A most artistic turn-out. It quite puts my uniform to shame.'

It had been the best meal of the voyage, at which even Broster had become faintly amiable. The Brigadier sat at the table looking natural in the scarlet tights and tail of Mephistopheles; Bill Coke, pink and hairy, wore nothing but a turkish towel pinned round his loins, and was sucking from a baby's bottle filled with Guinness; Gwenny had plaited her blonde hair and decked her sturdy limbs in the bright blue chintz of a china shepherdess; Mrs Judd wore the best bell-bottomed uniform of the slimmest quartermaster, commandeered by Ebbs; Mrs Lomax was a warmly veiled Salome; Dancer could do no better than his tennis flannels, and Willy Boast refused to let the serious progress of his evening be disturbed by such frippery as fancy clothes. Annette had come simply in her bra and pants as Jane, and Mrs Porteous was a nun.

'Quite an assembly,' Ebbs continued happily, looking round the unusually noisy passengers in the saloon, who had just reached the stage of throwing nuts at each other. 'I am really amazed that such talent – '

He was interrupted by a jubilant pop behind him.

'The champagne, sir,' Burtweed announced, as if ushering in a bishop.

'By Jove, bubbly!' said Dancer.

'My oath, plonk!' cried Bill Coke.

'My, my, gigglewater!' exclaimed Gwenny.

'I know a very interesting story about champagne,' said Brigadier Broster. 'I was staying in the country with some lord or other – I forget his name. He wasn't a very *rich* lord. In fact, he was a damnably poor lord. While I was there he heard he'd come into some money – not a lot, just ten or twenty thousand or so – and he thought we'd better celebrate. So he went to the cellar to look for some champagne. In England, of course,' he went on, swallowing half his glassful, 'we are very fond of champagne. We always keep some handy in our houses for birthdays and Christmas and so on. He found some champagne – a bottle of '19. He opened it. Flat as a pancake. Too old. So he opened a bottle of '20. Flat too. So was the '21, '22, '23, and '24. All flat. And the poor fellow had never been able to afford champagne since 1925. So we had to drink whisky and soda instead. Damn shame.' He finished the glass. 'Steward! More wine!'

'This is with the compliments of the Company,' Ebbs explained modestly. 'I hope you will all order lots more during the evening.'

'Do you know what, Captain?' Bill Coke said. 'We've had the finest time of our lives in this ship, and no mistake. Haven't we, Gwenny? And who have we got to thank for that? Why – you, Captain!'

'Hear, hear!' cried Mrs Judd loyally.

'Oh, come, come…'

Two or three of the passengers started beating on the table with their spoons.

'It's going to be a real shame to leave the *Charlemagne*. A real bloody shame,' Bill Coke continued, plunging abruptly into melancholy. 'Just think of it – a few hours from now, and we'll have packed our bags, gone down the gangway, and be scattered all over the shop. Never will we see each other again. That's what I call real sad, Gwenny.'

Gwenny touched her eyes quickly. 'I wish – I wish we could just go on living together like this for ever. For ever and ever.'

Under the stimulation of the champagne and these intoxicating sentiments, the table applauded loudly.

'Come and stay with us in Sydney!' Bill Coke exclaimed, extending his naked fat hairy pink arms across the table. 'All of you! Any time of day or night. Just ask anyone in Sydney for Bill Coke. They'll see you right.'

'Stay a week, or stay a month!' Gwenny excitedly tossed her pigtails over her shoulders like the *Charlemagne's* stern mooring ropes. 'Stay a year if you like!'

'But you must come and stay with us,' purred Mrs Porteous. 'I absolutely insist. We'll all have lots and lots to talk about.'

'Dash it!' Dancer blushed and glanced jerkily round the table. 'If you're back in London next year, I'd love to put you up. Be delighted. Absolutely delighted. I'm in the book.'

'Any time you're in Town,' Brigadier Broster declared gruffly. 'I'd be pleased if you'd come and dine. You can reach me through the Carlton.'

A squall of scribbling struck the table as they exchanged addresses. The irritations, squabbles, and jealousies of a voyage always sink in coastal waters: the passengers were now genuinely sorry to be losing each other's company, and autographed each decorated menu with lavish compliments.

'Ladies and gentlemen,' called Bill Coke. 'I'm going to propose a toast. Guess who? Why, the bloke who's done a damn fine job. The feller who's a real gent through and through. The Pommy I'd take my hat off to any time. Ladies and gents – the Captain!'

'Hooray!' cried Mrs Judd, clapping wildly.

'Captain– ' Bill Coke looked at Ebbs. 'I don't know how we'd have got on without you.' He suddenly climbed up on his chair, and for a second Ebbs thought he was about to make another scene. But instead he waved his table-napkin violently above his head, and the band in the corner paused, rearranged their rhythm, and struck up *For He's a Jolly Good Fellow.*

'Three cheers for the Captain!' shouted Bill Coke, now beginning to glisten all over. 'Three cheers for the Captain, everyone! Hip-hip-hip – '

The whole saloon rose and cheered. The passengers stood on their chairs, a few climbed on the tables, they threw streamers, waved paper hats, stamped, clapped, whistled, and began chanting: Speech! Speech! Speech!

Ebbs stood shakily. He opened his mouth and tried to say something. Instead, he blew his nose. His soul was skipping across bright waves of happiness like a flying fish.

After dinner Ebbs opened the ball.

It was still warm enough for dancing to be held on the saloon deck, which was specially decorated with flags and Chinese lanterns and partitioned by the buffet and a replica of the *Charlemagne* in iced cake six feet long. To a fusillade of champagne corks the fun began: soon Zulu was clutching flower-girl, clergyman holding chambermaid, schoolboy dancing with concubine, and sheik with char. The ship's junior officers streamed from their cabins down below, for the evening traditionally waived the regulation forbidding them, on pain of instant dismissal, from speaking to lady passengers about anything unconnected with the urgent safety of the ship. The steward's trays came heavily from the bar, the band played with an enthusiasm matching their record collection of free drinks hidden beneath the piano, the passengers began to blow squeakers and shout, the lanterns bobbed wildly, the balloons bounced playfully overhead, and the deck began to vibrate with gaiety. And all round there was nothing, except the sharks.

'Dear, dear William!' Mrs Judd said, as Ebbs jerkily propelled her through the thin first crop of dancers. 'What a wonderful evening!'

'Dear Edith! Do you know, this has been quite the happiest day of my life.'

She squeezed his arm. 'You're such a success, William! I'm terribly proud of you.'

'I have something I wish to say to you,' he declared, as the music stopped. He had decided it was high time to tell her about Burtweed's photograph.

133

'Have you, William?' She looked at him with surprise.

In his bath he had prepared a short speech, beginning with the photo and then proceeding warily by dead reckoning. But its delivery obviously needed solitude, and preferably darkness.

He blew his nose. 'Shall we try and find a spot on the deck?'

They began moving towards the rail, Ebbs beaming at the passengers like the vicar at a successful school treat. 'How happy everyone looks!' he observed contentedly, catching sight of Canon Swingle in a fez, popping balloons with a lighted cigar. 'There are indeed few sad hearts on board tonight.'

But one of the sad hearts was then beating anxiously on the bridge. Shawe-Wilson leant alone over the windcheater, frowning towards the dark bows. He rarely appeared there at all at sea, believing that the dull routine of navigation was more fittingly left to his junior officers; but now it had become his only sanctuary from Mrs Porteous.

He cursed softly into the gentle wind. He had only himself to blame for a bad error of judgement. He had thought of her as a mature woman who could start and stop an affair as easily as the engine of her car, and now the bloody female had fallen in love with him. She dogged him on deck, sneaked unwanted to his cabin at night, and splashed after him into the swimming-pool as eagerly as an otter-hound. Worse than that: only his most energetic charm had prevented her already sending her husband in Fremantle a cable telling him not to wait.

'I suppose the Old Man's fixed up for the night?' Jay said cheerfully, appearing at the wheelhouse door with a tin of cigarettes.

Shawe-Wilson grunted.

'By George, I wish I was you, Chief,' Jay went on brightly. 'I wouldn't be standing up here. No jolly fear, I wouldn't!' Shawe-Wilson was popular with his juniors, through being far too lazy to worry if they did any work or not. 'As soon as I'm off watch I'll be down there shaking a foot. You bet I will! What do you think of the turn-out?' He had renounced his afternoon sleep to take his turn with the officers' electric iron, and wore a white uniform as crisp as folded paper, which he inspected closely every few minutes in the chartroom light lest it had become contaminated with rust or paintwork.

'You look very beautiful,' Shawe-Wilson said sourly.

'You know, Chief,' Jay went on, becoming serious. 'I'm glad you've come up. I was going to ask you for some advice. You know all about – well, women, and things, don't you? I mean – well, everyone knows you do. You see – ' He rubbed his hands together slowly. 'You see, Chief. I've met a lovely little girl on board. A real smasher. But a – a spiritual sort of smasher, if you get what I mean. She sits at the Old Man's table. Her name's Annette. I meet her every morning when I'm sticking up the noon position in the Square. We haven't actually – actually spoken, you know. Company Regs and all that. But she's obviously a jolly decent girl. Jolly decent.'

'Never,' said Shawe-Wilson forcefully, 'have anything whatever to do with women at sea.'

'But Chief – !' Jay looked at him with amazement. 'I mean, there are lots of jolly nice women at sea, aren't there? I mean – well, clean, genuine sort of girls. Not – not *your* sort of women, Chief. I mean – I don't mean – well, that is, the sort of girls a chap can – sort of love, you know. Do you get me, Chief?' he asked desperately. 'What should I do about Annette?'

'Kick the little bitch's bottom over the side,' Shawe-Wilson said.

Feeling he could stand Jay no longer he went down the ladder towards the party. He stood on the edge of the dance floor, a cigarette in his mouth and his hands in his pockets, his dancing pumps weighed heavily with melancholy. Mrs Porteous was still not in sight; but he knew sure enough that she would soon appear on deck, and come trotting after him bubbling over with endearments.

'What a bloody life!' he groaned to himself. He realised sadly the penalties of being so handsome and so charming.

Looking round, he noticed a plain girl dressed as a Red Cross nurse, who had been staring at him shamelessly from the edge of the floor for some time. To take his mind off his problem and treat himself to the pale flattery of making her evening unforgettable, he asked on an impulse: 'May I give you a dance?'

She fell into his arms with a sigh.

'You must think me terribly, terribly silly,' she said, as soon as he started spinning her expertly across the floor. 'But – well, I just can't believe it.'

'Believe what?'

'Why, with all those girls on board I never thought for a moment you'd ever take any notice of poor little me.'

'Not a bit,' Shawe-Wilson said automatically, trying not to yawn. 'As a matter of fact, my dear, I've been simply itching for a chance to dance with you ever since we left London. But of course, I have to get round everybody somehow.'

'Have you really?' She looked at him excitedly. 'Wanted to dance with me, I mean? Do you know what I've hoped and dreamed about? All the voyage – ever since Tilbury. I've just been wanting you to say something to me. A word or a smile – that's all. Nothing more. Just as you were passing by on the deck. And now…and now you're actually dancing with me! Isn't it wonderful?'

'Where do you live in England?' he asked, feeling he ought to change the subject.

'In Warwickton. I bet you've never even heard of it.'

'Yes, I have,' he said politely, closely inspecting over her shoulder any other girls in sight. 'There's a castle there or something, isn't there?'

'Yes, that's where we live.'

'So you said, my dear. In Warwickton.'

'No, in the castle.'

'Oh, yes?' Shawe-Wilson immediately restricted his gaze to her face.

'Daddy bought it last year. It's near all his factories and things in Birmingham.'

'It's terribly silly of me, but I've forgotten your name for the second… '

'It's Sally – Sally Pritchett.'

'I suppose no relation to Pritchett's motors…?'

'Yes, Daddy does make a lot of cars. But all sorts of other things besides, of course.'

'I believe I've met your brother,' he said, trying to keep step.

'But I'm an only child!'

'Your parents? Are they well?'

She sighed. 'Mummy's very poorly these days. That's why I'm bringing her home from Australia.'

'And your father?'

'Poor dear Daddy! The doctor says he could drop dead any minute. There! The music's stopped! What a shame. Now you'll have to go.'

Shawe-Wilson took her firmly by the hand. 'You shall have the next dance, my dear. And the one after that. And the next. And the one following. It's not every night I have the chance of dancing with the most beautiful woman on board.'

'Beautiful?' She looked at him in astonishment. 'But I'm not really *beautiful.*'

'To me,' he said, 'you are the most beautiful woman in the world. Let's have a look at the boat-deck in the moonlight, shall we?'

He glanced at his watch. It was already eleven. The *Charlemagne* was due off Fremantle the following midnight, and he had Mrs Porteous to settle as well. He would have to hurry.

Ebbs was meanwhile having less luck with his courting. That night the boat-deck was bright with fairy-lights and noisy with couples, and he had just squeezed Mrs Judd into a shady space between the paint store and the engine-room hatchway and blown his nose, when Canon Swingle and his female gymnasts sought them out and hilariously dragged him back to their table on the dance floor. Remembering he had a duty to the ship, Ebbs obediently sat down and recommended the champagne, while Mrs Judd stroked his hand under cover of the paper foliage. After the gymnasts Ebbs was greeted by a succession of passengers, until at midnight he found himself sitting between McBride and Toddy, who were blowing squeakers, whistling at the girls, and calling each other chummie.

'I fear we have been somewhat frustrated,' Ebbs said to Mrs Judd, as she finished a dance with Earnshaw. He began leading her purposefully towards a well-thought-out niche behind the fire-alarm gear. 'It so happens that I had – ah, something particular to tell you, Edith, dear. Something that I – ah, thought I ought to tell you, as it were.'

'Yes, William?' She looked at him, her eyes shining.

'You see,' he said, manoeuvring her round the funnel. 'It's like this. I – well, you see. That photograph… '

'Captain! Captain! Where the devil's the Captain?' Brigadier Broster's voice roared faintly above the music.

'Oh, dear!' Ebbs groaned.

'Don't take any notice of him.' Mrs Judd gripped his arm.

'Where in blazes has the Captain got to? Where is he? Just let me get hold of the Captain – '

'I think I'd better go,' Ebbs said nervously. 'You never know what he might be up to.'

'Har!' exclaimed Broster, as Ebbs reappeared under the Chinese lanterns. 'And what is the meaning of this latest piece of blackguardry?'

Ebbs was too astonished to reply.

'Lining your pocket at the Company's expense, eh, Captain?' Broster's face began to suffer little twitches.

'I have not the slightest idea what you are talking about,' Ebbs said, becoming angry himself. 'But it hardly seems that your language is befitting a gentleman. Not to say slanderous. I will remind you, Brigadier, that the laws of land apply just as strictly at sea – '

'And so they do, Captain! And so they do! Look at that!' he pushed a champagne bottle under Ebbs' nose. 'Smell it!' he hissed. 'Sniff it! Taste it! Swallow it!'

'Why? What's wrong with it?'

'Wrong with it? Coke – a glass!'

Bill Coke, standing shamefacedly in his bath towel behind him, passed an empty champagne glass from the table.

'On your recommendation,' Broster continued, as though issuing commands to a firing-squad, 'I ordered – and paid for – Veuve Cliquot '47. And what do I get? Cider, damn it, or I'm a Dutchman!'

'But it's impossible!' cried Mrs Judd, standing faithfully at Ebbs' side. 'It's an outrageous suggestion!'

'Try it, then, madam! Try it!'

She took a sip.

'Well, madam? Well?'

She said nothing, and looked anxiously at Ebbs. 'It is cider,' she whispered.

'There! I told you so! What did I say? It's nothing but barefaced – '

'Quiet, quiet!' Ebbs shouted. He felt the *Charlemagne* was suddenly disintegrating round him. 'I assure you it's only some perfectly genuine mistake. They've got the labels mixed up, that's all. The Purser will put it right in a second. Where's the Purser? Where's Mr Prittlewell? Who's seen the Purser? Why, he was here just a minute ago. He can't be very far away.'

'Yes,' said Broster. 'That's the question. Where is the Purser?'

Ebbs found Prittlewell and Scottie hiding in the small locker behind the bar used for storing glasses.

'This is extraordinary behaviour, Purser,' said Ebbs, breathing heavily. 'quite unlike you, I must say. Running away when I need your support the most. A remarkable thing has happened – the champagne has got mixed up with the cider.'

'Scottie made an unfortunate mistake,' Prittlewell said, polishing his monocle nervously.

'That's just what I told them,' Ebbs said. 'But I must say, it's a very difficult one to explain.'

'It's all my fault.' Scottie sat down miserably on a case of gin. 'Gawd! After all these years. Fancy making a slip up like that!'

'Well you must do something about it at once. Open some bottles of cider – possibly they're full of champagne.'

'I said I was getting old, Herbie, didn't I?' Scottie shook his head. 'I should never have palmed off the cider on the old gaffer. Any barman half my age would have seen he was a regular champagne drinker.'

'Looks as though you did make a bit of a mess of it, Jim,' Prittlewell admitted.

'I'm sorry, Herbie. Honest, I am! We were doing a treat, too – good three hundred nicker in the kitty. And all that work I put in on them bottles! Ah, well.' He mopped his forehead with his glass-cloth. 'One lives and learns I suppose.'

'Don't take it to heart, Jim,' Prittlewell consoled him. 'There's always the next time.'

'Just one minute, if you please.' Ebbs had been following the conversation with interest. 'Do you mean – am I to understand that you served the passengers with cider – deliberately?'

'Be your age,' Prittlewell said wearily. 'You don't think we come to sea for our health, do you?'

'How dare you, Mr Prittlewell! How dare you, sir! I will remind you that you have committed a most serious – extremely serious – offence. Which I assure you will not go unpunished. No, indeed! Not for a moment. You will pay for this evening, most severely. I shall not have the slightest hesitation in bringing you both before the criminal authorities directly we touch Fremantle. Don't think you can expect any mercy from me. I will not have the slightest breath of impropriety…'

'I shouldn't be in too much of a hurry to have us locked up,' Prittlewell said. 'You're in this as much as we are, you know.'

'Me? Ridiculous! How?'

'You seem to have forgotten that your signature appears all over the account books. If anyone asks me, I'll tell them you were in with us. Lock, stock, and barrel.'

'Mr Prittlewell!' shouted Ebbs, turning pale. 'You wouldn't dare.'

'I certainly would. We're all – er, in the same boat, aren't we?'

'I will not yield to your threats,' Ebbs said. 'I will not – not for one moment.'

Prittlewell shrugged his shoulders. 'I wonder what you're going to do instead?'

Ebbs stared at him, at a loss for words.

There was a crash outside. Scottie briefly opened the locker door and whispered, 'Gawd! They're breaking up the bar!'

'Well, the captain will stop them,' Prittlewell said calmly.

'I certainly will not!'

'Go on, Captain. Mutiny and disorders on board are your job. You can explain away the champagne at the same time.'

'Mr Prittlewell, if you think – !'

Another crash and shouting from outside interrupted him. The excited passengers were now climbing over the unattended bar and helping themselves.

'Go along, Captain,' Prittlewell said gently.

'Blast you, Mr Prittlewell!'

Ebbs squeezed out of the locker and jumped on to the bar counter against the torrent of dancers. 'Wait!' he shouted desperately. 'Ladies and gentlemen! Please! Please! I have an important announcement – I implore you! Just one minute! Listen to reason –' No one took any notice of him. 'Please, ladies and gentlemen! I really must ask you in the name of reason to listen. Just for one second. Respect Company property, please. I can explain everything. Absolutely everything. I –' Someone playfully squirted a soda-siphon over him. 'God damn and blast you!' he cried, suddenly losing his temper. 'God blast the bloody lot of you! Go and wreck the bloody bar! Go and sink the bloody ship! Go and jump over the side, the whole bloody crowd of you! As far as passengers are concerned, I'd rather carry cattle!'

Wiping his hair with his handkerchief, he jumped on the deck, knocked two men out of his path, and strode despairingly to his cabin.

21

Ebbs sat at his desk, experiencing the sad relief of a freshly convicted criminal. The hopeless struggling and subterfuges were over, and now he had only to compose his soul as nobly as possible for his punishment. As a passenger captain he was a disastrous failure. Within an hour of Broster's certain cable reaching London another would be on its way telling him that his services were no longer required; and within a few minutes of stepping ashore at Tilbury he could be led away manacled to a policeman, dumped in a Black Maria, taken to the Old Bailey, and tried for embezzlement.

'So much for Captain Ebbs,' he sighed. How bitterly he wished he'd stayed in the homely *Martin Luther!*

He looked up and found Burtweed standing in the doorway with a tray.

'I brought you a bite of supper, sir,' he said softly.

'A kind thought, Burtweed. But I fear I am not hungry.'

'I also have a message from the madam, sir. She wishes to know if you'd care to see her.'

Ebbs shook his head. 'Please say that...that I appreciate the thought. But just now I should prefer to be alone. I shall look forward to seeing her in the morning. To say farewell,' he added. What was the point of saying anything else, when he had nothing to offer her but his chains?

'Very good, sir,' Burtweed said gently.

'It has been a somewhat unfortunate evening,' Ebbs continued remorsefully. 'I have behaved very foolishly. Losing my temper like that.'

'I'm real sorry, sir. Real proper sorry, I am. There's no one I'd be more sorry to see up the creek than you, sir. And that's straight.'

'It had to come sooner or later, I suppose. We find our limitations in the end, Burtweed.'

'Is there anything what I can do, sir? To help?'

'It is quite possible that you will be obliged to pack my few belongings in Fremantle. By this time tomorrow I might well be relieved of my command. Mr Shawe-Wilson, who I suppose is at least honest, will no doubt be promoted to this cabin. And I – ' He lowered his eyes. 'I shall be sent home, in disgrace.'

'No, sir! Never!'

'Disgrace is all I deserve.' He picked up his modest mermaid and pushed it round the desk slowly. 'I hope, Burtweed, that as far as you have been concerned I have been a good and just Captain?'

'Never a better, sir!'

'Thank you, Burtweed. Such words do not come amiss at the time. I shall see that your services are suitably recommended to the Company. Not that, I fear, my recommendation will carry much weight.'

'May I – ' Burtweed bit his lip. 'May I wish you the very best of luck, sir? With the greatest respect, sir?'

'Thank you, Burtweed.'

They shook hands solemnly.

'And I'm – I'm sorry I was cross, sir. About the madam, sir.'

'All is forgiven,' said Ebbs, with the serenity of an accomplished martyr.

'Thank you, sir. I knew you'd understand, sir.'

'Now, Burtweed, I must put a few of my affairs in order. I have many – ah, trials ahead.'

'Good night, sir.'

'Good night, Burtweed.'

When he was alone, Ebbs' drew a sheet of ship's writing-paper from his desk, dipped his pen in his horseshoe ink-stand, and began drafting a letter.

'Dear Sir Angus,' he wrote. 'It is with regret that I tender my resignation from the Company…'

He looked at this for some minutes, then added, 'in obedience to your

143

urgent cable of today's date'.

He paused, and stared gloomily at the tip of his nib. He wondered how he was going to earn a living ashore. He was forty-two, with no accomplishments beyond a capacity for navigating large ships round the world in open waters. He tried to remember the present employment of other unfortunate Captains: one was a seaside pier attendant, another sold boot polish at the door, and a third had some vaguely policing position with a row of bathing huts. Then he suddenly felt a draught of cold comfort from remembering that he would at least be freed from the problems of employment for several years to come, owing to imprisonment.

There was a knock on the door.

'Yes, Mr Jay?' he said discouragingly.

'I'm – I'm terribly sorry to bother you, and all that, sir. Terribly sorry, sir,' Jay stood stiffly at the stormstep, his cap tight under his arm, pressing his left toe into the deck with his right heel. 'You see, sir. Well, sir. I rather thought – '

'What is it man, what is it!'

'I was sort of well, actually, thinking of getting married, sir,' Jay explained, staring in front of him. 'And I thought, sir, that as you had nothing to do just at the moment you might be able to – sort of perform the ceremony, sir – ' He jumped back with a yell as Ebbs threw the inkpot at him, and went and locked himself in the officers' lavatory.

Ebbs continued his letter in pencil. After he had covered a page and a half there was another rap on the door.

'Go away!'

'…I assure you, sir, my greatest crime has been trusting my fellow men,' he wrote, frowning at the paper.

The knock was repeated.

'Yes, yes! What the devil is it now?'

Willy Boast was in the doorway. His face was pale, his hand shook on the handle. He opened his mouth, tried to speak, and staggered into the cabin.

'Man overboard!' he gasped.

'You're drunk!'

'No I'm not! Not very, anyway. There's someone overboard – the lady at our table.'

'Good God! Mrs Judd?" For a second Ebbs imagined that she had performed a conveniently appropriate form of suttee.

'No, no. The other. Mrs Porteous.' Willy East fell into a chair and held his head in his hands. 'I saw everything – everything! I couldn't get a drink because of that rumpus round the bar. I went on deck. She was there – standing by the rail, crying her eyes out. The poor child!'

'Crying?' Ebbs felt Mrs Porteous' soul would have to be drilled deeply to strike tears.

Willy Boast nodded, and two large sympathetic drops splashed on to the letter of resignation. 'She was dressed like a nun.'

Ebbs suddenly began to feel worried.

'She said…she said she had a broken heart. She was going to cast herself into the deep. Those were her very words. When I came back she was gone. Gone.'

There was another knock on the door. The fat Quartermaster stood outside with a nun's coif and veil.

'This is about the ruddy limit!' Ebbs exclaimed. His first thought was that it was typically inconsiderate of Mrs Porteous to commit suicide when he already had so much on his hands. 'Very well, we must search the ship, I suppose,' he said, instinctively reaching a swift decision. 'I am still the Captain, and I have my duty to everyone on board.' He threw his pencil aside, stood up, and reached for his cap. 'You will accompany me to the bridge, Mr Boast.'

'Don't happen to have a nip about you, do you?'

'I certainly do not. Quartermaster – kindly fetch the Chief officer.'

'Aye aye, sir.'

Willy Boast went to sleep with his head on the chart table and started to snore. Mrs Porteous' cabin was reported empty, her black nylon nightdress still neatly laid across the turned-down sheet. By then, Ebbs was sufficiently alarmed to call out the watch below, summon Brickwood and Bowles, and order them to search the ship.

'And where,' he said, 'the bloody hell is the blasted Chief Officer?'

'In his cabin, sir,' said the Quartermaster.

'Then why the devil didn't you give him my message? Haven't I had enough to put up with tonight already? Has *everyone* gone crazy?'

'I did give it, sir. He said to tell you he was occupied, and to say he'd be along when he could manage.'

Shawe-Wilson appeared in the chartroom ten minutes later, scowling heavily.

'Mr Shawe-Wilson,' Ebbs asked. 'Where have you been?'

'What's that got to do with you?'

'I will remind you – Take that blasted lipstick off your face!'

Shawe-Wilson sulkily wiped his cheek. 'Mr Shawe-Wilson, the present moment is too urgent even for me to give you the reprimand that you so richly deserve. And certainly will get. It happens that Mrs Porteous has most probably committed suicide by jumping from the ship.'

'What!'

'Yes, Mr Shawe-Wilson,' Ebbs continued forcefully. 'I thought that would upset you. When did you last see her alive?'

'Why – I spoke to her on deck about midnight,' he said, looking frightened.

'Did you have – ah, words?' Shawe-Wilson was silent. 'Did you?' Ebbs shouted.

'Well, we did have a sort of a tiff,' he admitted.

'Aha! That will go badly against you at the court of inquiry, Mr Shawe-Wilson!'

'I should think you won't look too good,' Shawe-Wilson snapped. 'After all, she's been to your cabin.'

'Oh, you know about that, do you?'

'Yes, I do. I only kept quiet about it to please her.'

Ebbs blew his nose loudly. 'Mr Shawe-Wilson,' he continued, 'tonight I have had many trials to bear. I have been accused of robbery in public, blackmailed in private, and exposed to the ridicule of the entire Pole Star Line by losing my temper before a babble of drunken passengers armed with soda siphons. As all these events will certainly result in my dismissal from the Company as soon as the necessary cables are exchanged with London, I have the small compensation that I can stop treating my officers with the gentlemanly consideration I have foolishly afforded them during the voyage. Mr Shawe-Wilson, you are an unspeakable slimy blackguard, who is not fit to collect the tickets for deck-chairs on a paddle-steamer to Margate. I have no doubt whatever that you will come to a sticky end, and I only hope that I shall have the satisfaction of reading about it in the Sunday papers. As you are useless for any duties concerned with the navigation and conduct of the ship, you might as well go below and continue your lechery with the poor woman who I have no doubt you are concealing there.'

'Look here – !'

'That is all, Mr Shawe-Wilson.'

'I won't be spoken to by a third-rate tramp-ship Captain – !'

'Quartermaster! Escort Mr Shawe-Wilson from the bridge!' Ebbs blew his nose again. 'Good night, Mr Shawe-Wilson!' After all, he thought, there were some advantages in being sacked.

There was no sign of Mrs Porteous.

'Very well,' Ebbs said firmly. 'We shall have to reverse course. Mr Brickwood!'

'Sir?'

'Kindly give Sparks our position and tell him to wireless all ships in the neighbourhood to keep a sharp look out for a nun.'

The *Charlemagne* swept back in a circle, extra lookouts clattered urgency down the ladders towards the fo'c'sle head, and Ebbs paced the bridge in silence wondering with increasing force if he ought to follow his passenger over the rail. The officers gloomily watched the black water beyond the narrow streaks of the bow waves. Everyone on the bridge knew the search was hopeless and conducted only out of respect for the log-book and the court of inquiry, for by then Mrs Porteous had certainly been carried away beneath the fin of a contented shark.

Before dawn, Ebbs said wearily to Brickwood, 'I'm turning in. I think I've had about as much as I can stand for today.'

'Very good, sir.'

'Resume course in half an hour. Call me if you see anything. Call me anyway at five, and I shall cable the Company. I thank you, gentlemen, for your services,' he continued dejectedly to the two officers. 'They will be given credit in the log-book. Though after this disastrous day I fear it will be the last act I shall perform in this or any other vessel.'

The two Mates exchanged sad glances, then Ebbs went slowly down the ladder, leaving them saluting at the top as if he were a corpse disappearing into its grave.

Poor Mrs Porteous! he thought as he made for his cabin. She wasn't a bad sort at heart. And someone at least was worse off than he was. Though in twenty-four hours the lights of Fremantle would be dancing round their bows, and God knows what there was in store for him behind them.

He opened his cabin door. He stopped, his hand on the light switch. He heard a noise. 'Not again… ' he muttered.

He turned on the light. Priscilla was sitting at his desk in her nightdress, eating his supper.

'Well God bless my sweet Aunt Fanny!' Ebbs exclaimed.

She dropped her eyes, and looked penitently at the bitten half of a cheese sandwich.

'I'm hungry,' she explained.

'Oh, you are, are you?' Ebbs said. 'And let me tell you, my girl, that this time you have gone too far. Much too far! Do you realise it is extremely dangerous for little girls to wander about the ship in the middle of the night like this? With practically nothing on, too,' he added primly. 'What would your mummy and daddy have to say, may I ask?'

'They're blotto,' she told him.

'That's nothing to do with it.'

'They wouldn't let me have any supper,' she said. 'Because I was sick.'

'I should think not!'

'I – I wasn't *very* sick.' She looked at him steadily for a moment, then suddenly began to cry.

'Now, now, now, little girl! You mustn't cry. Not here, anyway. You must go back to your cabin. All right, you can finish your cheese sandwich if you like. I'll wrap the rest up in the doily and you can take it with you. But please try and stop making that filthy noise.'

She went on howling.

'For God's sake shut up!' Ebbs yelled. 'Or I'll kick your beastly little teeth in!'

She stopped, and stared at him in amazement.

'And how the devil did you get up here anyway?' he demanded.

'The lady sent me,' she said meekly.

'Lady? Which lady?'

'The lady that thinks you're cold.'

'What!' Ebbs crouched down beside her. 'Are you sure? Where is she?'

'I won't tell you.'

'Priscilla! Please!' he pleaded. 'When did you see her? Where? Tell me, there's a good girl.'

She bit her lower lip.

'Priscilla! I'm your friend, aren't I? You remember me don't you? I'm the Captain.'

'You were nasty to me,' she told him. 'I don't like you.'

'But – but don't you remember, I gave you half a crown?' Ebbs said desperately. 'Please, Priscilla! Think of all those lovely cream buns and things at the party. We were great pals, weren't we? Just tell me where the lady is – and then... And then I'll wake up the Chief Steward, and you shall have ice-cream and sausages and pickled walnuts and éclairs and anything you want and as much as you like,' he promised lavishly. 'See? On my word of honour, Priscilla.'

She looked at him carefully, judging whether to forgive him or not: for a second she held his future in her sticky little hands. Then she slipped off his chair.

'I'll show you,' she said. Ebbs followed her on to the deck, down the ladders, and into the passenger accommodation. She skipped along the empty alleyway ahead of him, turned the corner, and stopped.

'There!' she pointed.

It was a cabin door.

'Are you sure?'

She nodded. Ebbs knocked. There was no reply. He rattled the handle.

It was locked.

'This is the Captain,' he called. 'Open up!'

Silence.

He pushed the door with his shoulder, kicked it open, and switched on the light.

'Why, bless my soul!' he exclaimed. Suddenly he began to laugh. 'Well, well!' he said. 'Talk of the devil!'

22

'We are men of the world,' said Brigadier Broster.

'Oh, quite,' Ebbs agreed cheerfully. 'Men of the world.' It was almost noon the next day. The *Charlemagne* was forcing herself at two extra knots across a bright calm sea, barely twelve hours away from port. Ebbs was sitting in his cabin, his feet on his desk, a look of contentment on his face, and his hands clasped comfortably across his stomach.

Broster took a cigar-case from his pocket.

'Smoke, Captain?'

'Thank you.'

'At sea,' Brigadier Broster went on, offering Ebbs a match, 'a certain – shall we say? – lack of convention…a certain *camaraderie,* a certain incitement to adventure, are almost traditional.'

'I agree perfectly,' Ebbs said.

'Better men than I, Captain,' Broster continued sombrely, 'far better men, have fallen under the magical spell of the ocean night.'

'Of course.'

'Which I'm sure you'll agree, Captain, is highly conducive to feelings of an irresponsible nature.'

Ebbs nodded. 'So it seems.'

There was a pause. Broster looked at his cigar as if trying to identify some strange object.

'A degree of discretion, Captain… '

'Ah, discretion!'

'A man in your position must surely feel a sense of responsibility about such things. After all, a captain of a ship at sea is the repository of many confidences. Willing and unwilling. And what goes unrevealed about a man, Captain,' he added with emphasis, 'is often of much greater importance than what is said.'

'Much greater,' Ebbs observed, blowing smoke towards the deckhead.

'Well now.' Brigadier Broster beamed at him. 'Surely we can come to some understanding?'

Ebbs took his feet off the desk. 'Brigadier Broster,' he began briskly. 'The fact that I discovered you with a woman in your cabin is not a matter that obliges me to make an official report. Though no doubt the story would – because of your important position in the Line – make something of a stir if it was given out.'

'Certainly,' Broster said heartily. 'I'm not denying it.'

'Not to mention the effect it might have on your wife. Who I believe will be waiting for you on the quay at Fremantle?'

'Ah, yes,' Broster went on thoughtfully. 'I should certainly prefer the story to stay away from her ears. Mrs Broster would be deeply distressed at hearing about my moment's foolishness – which was precipitated, I must insist, wholly through taking pity on a poor woman in tears.'

'I'm sure she would.'

'I think far too highly of my wife to submit her to such pain. Besides, she is a lady of extremely quick temper and might not be entirely responsible for her actions. No,' he decided, 'it would be best, Captain, for the little affair to remain a secret between us. Just a little secret. We have had our differences during the voyage, to be sure. But of course there was nothing personal in it. Not for one moment! It was the officer, not the man, that I occasionally criticised. I did so only because I had the Company's interests at heart. As you have yourself, I'm sure. But now all is forgiven and forgotten,' he went on more brightly. 'We are approaching our journey's end. Soon we shall be safely in port, with the troubles and trials of the voyage sunk behind us without trace. We must part as true good friends, Captain. I give you my hand.'

'One moment.' Ebbs drew thoughtfully on his cigar, ignoring Broster's eager palm. 'It so happens, Brigadier, that in this case matters have been somewhat taken out of my hands. It is not simply that you were – ah, chambering with a fellow passenger. At one-thirty last night the vessel was turned about on her course to search for this woman, for whom the alarm had already been raised, the watch below turned to, and the ship searched from truck to keel. The ship's log-book, Brigadier – ' He severely tapped the foolscap book in front of him with his forefinger. 'An official document, inspected every voyage by the shipping authorities in London, and perused minutely by Sir Angus himself. As Captain of the ship I am obliged by Act of Parliament to enter a full and truthful account of why we altered course last night, and also the reason for resuming it again. To omit or to falsify the facts makes me liable to severe penalties under the law. Not to mention my professional dishonour. I shall therefore be making the correct entry. Almost immediately.' Ebbs picked up his pen. 'Good day to you, sir.'

'One minute!' The ash shook loose from the end of Broster's cigar. 'Is it strictly necessary for you, Captain, to be absolutely explicit?'

'My conscience demands it.'

'But surely! Not every detail – '

'Every single one. Including the remarkable sight – '

'Captain,' Broster said earnestly. 'I am a man of vast influence in the Line. I don't have to tell you that. I have power that extends right into the boardroom, and beyond. I have the ability to bestow favours even beyond Angus McWhirrey himself.'

'Ah!' Ebbs said. 'Now you're talking.'

'What,' asked Broster, as if he were swallowing pieces of glass, 'can I do for you, Captain?'

'Have a seat,' Ebbs said. He picked up the pile of ship's notepaper on which the night before he had written his resignation. 'You have a pen? Good. All I wish you to do is write a letter. No,' Ebbs corrected himself. 'First of all, I want you to send a cable. I will dictate it.' He considered for a moment. ' "McWhirrey Binnicle, London," ' he said. ' "Magnificent voyage ship first class Captain excellent." Sign it "Broster." Don't worry,' he added as the Brigadier wrote out the words doubtfully. 'I shall pay the cost. Now for the letter. "Dear Angus – "That's how you usually address him?' Broster nodded. 'Good. "Dear Angus, I'm writing to let you know as soon as possible how highly I think of that fellow Ebbs." Ebbs blew his nose. ' "He has done a simply magnificent job. He has all the qualities of a fine passenger-ship Captain, and I certainly recommend that he be retained in the *Charlemagne* for the present. Afterwards, of course, he may be needed in one of our newer and larger ships." I'm not going too fast for you?' Ebbs asked.

'No,' muttered Broster.

' "Ebbs – " New paragraph, by the way. "Ebbs particularly won my respect for the way in which he tactfully dispersed a crowd of drunken passengers becoming unruly just before arriving in Fremantle. I also commend the energy with which he ferreted out the machinations – " Can you spell it? There's a dictionary in the desk.'

' "Scheming" might be better,' Broster grunted.

'Yes, scheming. "Scheming of the dishonest Purser and barman, whom I earnestly entreat you to deal with according to the terms of Captain Ebbs' report. An excellent fellow, Ebbs, with a brilliant future in the Company. I shall keep my eye on him."' Ebbs grinned, 'Sign it your usual way if you please. Address the envelope. I will post it myself.'

'If you should find yourself tempted to repudiate this letter at any time,' Ebbs continued pleasantly, as he blotted and folded the paper, 'remember the *Charlemagne's* log-book. I can make the necessary entry any time before we return to London.' He chuckled. 'Well, Brigadier, I see no reason why the warm friendship you envisaged between us a few minutes ago should not now come into being. We have quite a tie between us. We certainly have one thing in common, anyway.' He chuckled again. 'A private joke of my own – you wouldn't understand. Excellent cigars, these. Have you any more?'

'I'll send a box to your cabin,' Broster growled.

'Thank you. Perhaps we shall sail together again in the future…?'

The Brigadier rose. 'Captain Ebbs,' he said with deliberation, 'one thing you may be certain of: whatever your fate in the Company henceforward as a result of that piece of outrageous forgery – whether you end up in jail or, as I'm afraid is more likely, as the Line's Commodore – you may be sure of one thing. I shall make it my business never to set foot again in any ship with you in it. Good morning to you, sir!'

As soon as Broster had gone Ebbs began to roar with laughter, and when at last he looked up he found the Chief Radio Officer standing over him anxiously.

'What is it, Sparks?' he asked, wiping his face with his handkerchief and letting his mirth drain away in an eddy of chuckles.

'Cable for you, sir.'

'From Fremantle?'

'No, from London, sir.'

Ebbs opened it, still grinning. 'Sparks!' he called after him. 'Kindly present my compliments to Mr Shawe-Wilson and ask him to step into my cabin, if you please.'

Shawe-Wilson appeared with his hands in his pockets. He greeted Ebbs with a smirk and asked, 'You wanted me for something?'

'Certainly, Mr Shawe-Wilson. Come inside, please. I trust you have recovered your temper this morning?'

'That's a bit thick!' He sat on the edge of Ebbs' desk and helped himself to a cigarette. 'I for one managed to behave like a gentleman last night.'

'Mr Shawe-Wilson,' Ebbs said amiably. 'I will remind you that we are still in the same relationship in rank as we started the voyage. The friendliness you now demonstrate is most heartening, but I feel I really must ask you to behave a trifle more formally in your Captain's cabin.'

'Got a light?' Shawe-Wilson asked.

'Over there. Yes. I feel that nevertheless – '

'I shan't be with you much longer,' Shawe-Wilson interrupted. 'I'll be leaving the ship as soon as I sign off in London.'

'Really?'

'Yes, I'm getting married.'

'Congratulations.'

'I'm giving up the sea. I shall be living in Warwickton. Do you know it? My fiancée's got a castle there.'

'No, I have sadly neglected my beauty spots.'

'You must come and stay when we're settled.'

'I should be delighted.'

'We shall be married pretty soon,' Shawe-Wilson went on. 'My fiancée has altered her plans, and she'll be sailing home with us. It'll be a May wedding. I suppose at St George's, Hanover Square. There isn't anywhere else really, is there?'

Ebbs blew his nose. 'Mr Shawe-Wilson,' he said, 'I have no doubt you will do everything possible to marry this unfortunate girl sooner or later, but you will certainly not be doing so in May. I have a cable here from Leadenhall Street. I will read it to you: "Transfer Fremantle Chief Officer J R E M W Shawe-Wilson for voyages based Hong Kong until expiry articles SS *Martin Luther* arriving next month." '

Ebbs wondered for a second if he was going to be struck.

'It's a lie!' Shawe-Wilson shouted.

'Read it, my dear fellow.' Ebbs waved the paper playfully.

'It's a forgery!'

'Radio for confirmation if you wish. The rates are not high.'

'They can't do it! They've no right to!'

Ebbs put his feet on the desk again.

'Oh, but they can, Mr Shawe-Wilson. Company Regulations, you know. The articles you signed in this ship in London bind you to my command for a period of eighteen months. By the same articles, I am perfectly free to transfer you if I wish to any other ship in the Company. I simply act as I am directed by the head office. Obedience is the first requirement of a good officer – as I am sure you appreciate, Mr Shawe-Wilson.'

Shawe-Wilson angrily flung Ebbs' cigarette box on the deck.

'The *Luther* is for some reason short of a Chief Officer – possibly the last one died. It is quite on the cards in the *Luther* – she will now remain out East for at least two years, so you will be brought home when your articles expire in – let me see...' He looked at his hundred-years' calendar. 'Sixteen months and twenty-eight days. Then you will be able to claim your bride. If she has waited for you.' Ebbs pummelled his finger-tips together. 'Good day, Mr Shawe-Wilson. That will be all.'

23

Early on a bright Australian summer morning the *Charlemagne* left her anchorage in Gage Roads and floated slowly up the Swan river towards the landing-stage at Fremantle. On deck, most of the passengers stood ready to disembark, startling in their ordinary clothes. Their baggage was waiting in its slings below the derricks, down below the stewards were counting and comparing their tips, and the ship's band were battling bravely with their hangovers to strike up *Waltzing Matilda*. Unbelievably, the voyage was over.

The *Charlemagne* had left London almost unnoticed, but to the warm-hearted Australians to whom 'home' is always first a vision of England, foggy, green, cottage-spattered, over-policed, buttressed and turreted, her arrival was an event of almost national importance. Below the long poster WELCOME TO AUSTRALIA the simmering crowd threw streamers which fluttered prematurely on to the water, and as the amorphous mass of people on the rails began to crystallise into faces, they tried to shout greetings across the rowdy conversation that the ship was holding with her tugs. Soon the gangways pierced the *Charlemagne's* sides and her passengers began streaming down to the quay. After almost a month whose chief problem had been how to pass the time they faced again the familiar vexations of society, now represented by the Customs man, the passport officer, and the surly porter already complaining of the high cost of living and the insufficiency of tips.

'They fly forgotten as a dream,' Ebbs quoted sombrely. He was watching his passengers disembark, unseen in a corner of the bridge. He blew his nose with deep feeling.

'The madam is waiting, Sir,' said Burtweed, appearing up the ladder.

'Ah, good!' Ebbs immediately looked more cheerful. 'I shall wish to be undisturbed, Burtweed. For about half an hour. Is that understood?'

'Understood perfect, sir.'

Ebbs chuckled. 'And very soon, Burtweed, you shall have your photograph back.'

'Thank you, sir. It'll be nice to see it again. It's the only bit of brightness what we've got in our cabin.'

'I have been most grateful for it, but I'm glad to say it will shortly be – ah, somewhat out of date.' He looked at Burtweed coyly. 'For your kindness in lending it to me, Burtweed, I should like to make some recompense. Perhaps you would get yourself a case of beer from the bar and charge it to my account?'

'That's real kind of you, sir, but I never touch a drop at sea.'

'Well, a carton of cigarettes?'

'Nor smoke, sir.'

'Surely there's something you want? Anything, my dear fellow – just name it.'

'I could do badly with some more foot salts, sir.'

'Foot salts? Certainly. Order as much as you like from the barber's shop. I'll sign the chit.'

'You are very, very good, sir,' Burtweed said with feeling.

'Nonsense, Burtweed. It was the least I could do. I hope they will give you many hours of enjoyment. And now to my private business.'

'Alone at last!' he cried, bounding into his cabin and throwing his cap into the corner. 'Or almost, at any rate.'

'Dear William!' Mrs Judd was sitting pertly in the corner of his sofa. 'She's going to be a very quiet ship round to Sydney.'

'Ah, but you will be in her, my dear,' he said, sitting down beside her and taking her hand.

'You dear sweet darling!' She respectfully ruffled his hair.

'And now,' Ebbs said. He blew his nose twice. 'And now, I have something to say to you.'

'Yes, William?' She settled herself more comfortably.

'Edith, my dear. We have known each other a very short time. A very short time, in time. Ah – you follow?'

She nodded.

'But nevertheless, in the intimacy of shipboard life, we have come to know each other well. Extremely well. Remarkably, in fact.' He reached across the desk and picked up Burtweed's photograph solemnly. 'I'm going to begin, Edith, by making a confession.'

'Confession?' She looked surprised.

'Oh, not an unpleasant one, I assure you. On the contrary, a very pleasant one. One that, in fact, puts everything in quite a different light. Quite different. A light that, I must confess, I should like to have shed on things much earlier. You see, this is not really – Yes, Burtweed? What is it?' He looked up crossly as the Tiger pulled aside the door-curtain.

'Beg pardon, sir. But one of the passengers wants to say goodbye at the gangway.'

'Burtweed, I thought I told you distinctly I was not to be disturbed?'

'Pardon, sir. But it seemed special, sir.'

'Oh, all right.' Ebbs impatiently slipped the photograph into his pocket. 'Will you excuse me, Edith? I won't be a minute. Don't go away,' he added.

'I won't,' she said firmly.

'Who the devil is it?' Ebbs whispered, as he stepped from the cabin.

'Mrs Porteous, sir. I didn't like to say.'

'Quite right – quite right.'

'She sent a note to be delivered discreet, sir.'

Ebbs opened a folded piece of paper and read:

Captain dear

Aren't you going to say goodbye to a girl? I must see you. Absolutely vital. If you don't come I shall tell all!

EP.

'Where is she?' he asked nervously, screwing up the paper.

'By the first-class sally port, sir.'

'I'd better go, I suppose.'

Mrs Porteous, already hot in redundant mink, purred to him, 'Captain, I do so much want you to meet my husband.'

'And – ah, how do you do?' Ebbs said, shaking hands awkwardly. He had often tried to imagine Mrs Porteous' husband during the voyage, and had seen him vaguely as a mixture of Superman and Mr Anthony Eden. He turned out to be a sallow, fat, amiable fellow in thick spectacles and a check suit.

'Now run along and see to the baggage, darling,' Mrs Porteous said. 'I'll stay here and say goodbye to the Captain.'

When they were alone she smiled at Ebbs and said, 'I was a very naughty girl, wasn't I?'

'Well...you must admit, madam, there have been moments.'

'I could have screamed when I saw your face – the night you found me in your cabin.'

'Perhaps we needn't discuss that now?'

She laid a hand gently on his arm. 'I am the goddess of discretion.'

'I'm sure you have reason to be,' he said primly.

'Well, Captain,' she went on softly. 'You seem to have done well for yourself out of the voyage, in that respect.'

'Yes,' Ebbs agreed, warming to the conversation. 'I really believe I have.'

'Such a nice person, Edith Judd.'

'Very nice.'

'How silly to think,' Mrs Porteous went on, 'that we more or less tossed a coin for you at the beginning of the trip.' She sighed. 'And she won. Ah, well! I suppose my technique isn't what it was. Still, I bear her no malice.'

'I am gratified to hear it,' Ebbs said stiffly.

'After all, her need is so much greater than mine. She's getting on for thirty-eight – '

'Thirty-two. She told me so herself.'

'Did she? You know how long she's been widowed, of course?'

'Two years. She told me that, too.'

Mrs Porteous laughed softly. 'Oh, dear, no! Two months is nearer to it.

Her husband left her absolutely destitute, poor thing. Died of drink you know – you heard all about that? The widow's cruise… ' Mrs Porteous smiled. 'The oldest bait in the world, my dear. Of course, we knew you're not really married. The Brigadier always told us lots of things about you at breakfast. But I'm sure you'll be very, very happy,' she ended brightly. 'Now here's my husband. Goodbye, Captain. And thank you so much for an unforgettable trip.'

She left Ebbs frowning by the gangway. He walked slowly towards his cabin. He took out Burtweed's photograph and stared at it. Of course, Mrs Porteous was a most unreliable sort of woman, whose word should never be trusted. Still, she knew a great deal more about these things than he did. Her worldly opinions perhaps deserved some respect. And Mrs Judd had deliberately pretended to be taken in by his little deception. He paused abaft No.4 lifeboat. He blew his nose thoughtfully. Around him were the cranes, the warehouses, the roads, the fields, the hills of the hard-hearted land. A train whistle blew noisily just below, and the magic of the sea for a second skipped away. Perhaps he was really making a hasty decision? Surely nothing was more deceptive than a feverish shipboard courtship? He thought deeply for a minute or two. Then for the first time in his life he faced the future with confidence. He decided to say nothing more just yet. After all, he still had the trip to Sydney to make up his mind. Come to that, he thought with an exciting new wave of devilment, who knows what the voyage home might bring?

Richard Gordon

Doctor in the House

Richard Gordon's acceptance into St Swithin's medical school came as no surprise to anyone, least of all him – after all, he had been to public school, played first XV rugby, and his father was, let's face it, 'a St Swithin's man'. Surely he was set for life. It was rather a shock then to discover that, once there, he would actually have to work, and quite hard. Fortunately for him, life proved not to be all dissection and textbooks after all… This hilarious hospital comedy is perfect reading for anyone who's ever wondered exactly what medical students get up to in their training. Just don't read it on your way to the doctor's!

'Uproarious, extremely iconoclastic' – *Evening News*
'A delightful book' – *Sunday Times*

Doctor at Sea

Richard Gordon's life was moving rapidly towards middle-aged lethargy – or so he felt. Employed as an assistant in general practice – the medical equivalent of a poor curate – and having been 'persuaded' that marriage is as much an obligation for a young doctor as celibacy for a priest, he sees the rest of his life stretching before him. Losing his nerve, and desperately in need of an antidote, he instead signs on with the Fathom Steamboat Company. What follows is a hilarious tale of nautical diseases and assorted misadventures at sea. Yet he also becomes embroiled in a mystery – what is in the Captain's stomach-remedy? And, more to the point, what on earth happened to the previous doctor?

'Sheer unadulterated fun' – *Star*

RICHARD GORDON

DOCTOR AT LARGE

Dr Richard Gordon's first job after qualifying takes him to St Swithin's where he is enrolled as Junior Casualty House Surgeon. However, some rather unfortunate incidents with Mr Justice Hopwood, as well as one of his patients inexplicably coughing up nuts and bolts, mean that promotion passes him by – and goes instead to Bingham, his odious rival. After a series of disastrous interviews, Gordon cuts his losses and visits a medical employment agency. To his disappointment, all the best jobs have already been snapped up, but he could always turn to general practice…

DOCTOR GORDON'S CASEBOOK

'Well, I see no reason why anyone should expect a doctor to be on call seven days a week, twenty-four hours a day. Considering the sort of risky life your average GP leads, it's not only inhuman but simple-minded to think that a doctor could stay sober that long…'

As Dr Richard Gordon joins the ranks of such world-famous diarists as Samuel Pepys and Fanny Burney, his most intimate thoughts and confessions reveal the life of a GP to be not quite as we might expect… Hilarious, riotous and just a bit too truthful, this is Richard Gordon at his best.

RICHARD GORDON

GREAT MEDICAL DISASTERS

Man's activities have been tainted by disaster ever since the serpent first approached Eve in the garden. And the world of medicine is no exception. In this outrageous and strangely informative book, Richard Gordon explores some of history's more bizarre medical disasters. He creates a catalogue of mishaps including anthrax bombs on Gruinard Island, destroying mosquitoes in Panama, and Mary the cook who, in 1904, inadvertently spread Typhoid across New York State. As the Bible so rightly says, 'He that sinneth before his maker, let him fall into the hands of the physician.'

THE PRIVATE LIFE OF JACK THE RIPPER

In this remarkably shrewd and witty novel, Victorian London is brought to life with a compelling authority. Richard Gordon wonderfully conveys the boisterous, often lusty panorama of life for the very poor – hard, menial work; violence; prostitution; disease. *The Private Life of Jack The Ripper* is a masterly evocation of the practice of medicine in 1888 – the year of Jack the Ripper. It is also a dark and disturbing medical mystery. Why were his victims so silent? And why was there so little blood?

'…horribly entertaining…excitement and suspense buttressed with authentic period atmosphere' – *The Daily Telegraph*

Made in the USA
Lexington, KY
16 February 2014